Foreword by

Donald J. Trimp
President of the United States of America

This is the worst book I have ever read. I mean, it's absolute garbage. And if this book is published (won't happen) I will sue the author (who is a real punk and a big loser by the way) for defamation.

Look, I don't have the spare time to write forewords for unknown Canadian authors. I'm extremely busy running one of the largest empires the world has ever known. Plus, now, I'm the president of the United States of America, so, I'm like kind of double plus busy. And, I'm really, really good at it.

But, because I'm in the book, and the author sent me the manuscript, I felt obliged to read *The Mouse Who Poked an Elephant*. I mean, if you were famous enough that people wrote about you, would you read the stuff they wrote? Sure you would. And, if they wrote mean things about you, would you fire back? It's a rhetorical question.

Anyway, this is a terrible book. I mean what genre is it even? Speculative political fiction? Is that even a thing? The future me would never do or say half of the things this author writes about. And I am not a big threat to world peace or the global environment like this book says.

Listen carefully, Mark Piper: if you publish this book, I will sue you so hard you'll need to rent a room in Rosie O'Donnell's shed and sell all of your internal organs to pay me.

And YOU, if you are reading this foreword: don't you dare buy this book. Put it down, and walk away. That's it. Good decision. Oh, hey—my book is still on the shelves if you are looking for a great book to buy. It's called *The Art of the Steal* by Donald J. Trimp. It was a *New York Times* bestseller. That means millions of people bought my book. Millions of people don't make stupid choices, so it must be a true literary masterpiece. Not like this stupid Mouse and Elephant thing. Anyway, I gotta go drain swamps and make America Great. Again.

Donald J. Trimp
Bestselling Author of *The Art of the Steal*
CEO, Trimp, Inc.
POTUS

The Mouse Who Poked an Elephant

Book One of The Mouse and Elephant Trilogy

MARK PIPER

The Mouse Who Poked an Elephant
Copyright © 2017 by Mark Piper

No part of this publication may be reproduced, distributed, or transmitted in any form or by any means, including photocopying, recording, or other electronic or mechanical methods, without the prior written permission of the author, except in the case of brief quotations embodied in critical reviews and certain other non-commercial uses permitted by copyright law.

tellwell

Tellwell Talent
www.tellwell.ca

ISBN
978-1-77302-630-5 (Hardcover)
978-1-77302-631-2 (Paperback)
978-1-77302-629-9 (eBook)

Preface

The Mouse Who Poked an Elephant

In hindsight I should have asked someone other than Donald Trimp to write the foreword to my first novel. Nevertheless, if the function of a foreword is to have a famous person lend credibility to the author's work, then Mr. Trimp has provided tremendous value.

This book is about what could come to pass in the near future. Or not. I mean I'm not psychic or anything.

Like many of you, I just have some concerns about how we in the Western or developed world are currently conducting our affairs.

If you are a baby boomer, you have been fortunate enough to have lived (thus far) in a time of tremendous personal opportunity, political stability and financial prosperity. But should we as a demographic group expect that our current high standard of living is sustainable? If you think the answer to that question is yes, please introduce me to the people who are willing to pay for that.

Our current standard of living is not sustainable. We have harvested the earth's resources at a brutally efficient pace over the past fifty years. Essentially, baby boomers have raped the planet for profit, and managed to leave a tragic environmental legacy and crippling debt in our wake. Be honest. We need to change the way we think, act, work, consume and live.

So this story is a light-hearted look at how that change might come about. It's a tale about love and hate, life and death, young and old, rich and poor, money and politics, greed and generosity, capitalism and sustainability, trust and treachery…you know, just regular human drama we all experience in varying degrees.

I hope you find the story thought-provoking enough to buy it.

Oh, by the way—this is a work of fiction. Characters in the story resembling real people you may have heard of is purely coincidental.

Mark Piper
April 2017

Table of Contents

Chapter 1. We Play the Cards We Are Dealt 11
Chapter 2. Political Science 101 17
Chapter 3. Maybe Chicken Little Was Right…........... 35
Chapter 4. Hotter Than Hot... 49
Chapter 5. The Uncomfortable Pension
  Plan Dilemma 71
Chapter 6. Shaking Shit Up 83
Chapter 7. A Visit to SimpleTown 95
Chapter 8. A Snowball's Chance in Hell 129
Chapter 9. It Still Seems Unlikely 139
Chapter 10. Canada Did What Now? 151
Chapter 11. Unlikely Soldiers..................................... 165
Chapter 12. Pioneering... 179
Chapter 13. A Changing Nation 187
Chapter 14. A Cold Dark Winter 203
Chapter 15. Faint Hope Clause 225

Acknowledgments

This book would not have been possible without the love and support of my wife Elaine. It also never would have been started without inspiration and encouragement from my sons Brechin and Brendan Piper. *The Mouse Who Poked an Elephant* is dedicated to them, and to all people willing to embrace change.

A big shout out to the very talented Keith MacLeod of Dartmouth Nova Scotia for the cover illustration. Last but not least, endless gratitude to the team at Tellwell Publishing for their tireless and patient efforts in guiding a new author through the publishing process.

Canadians and the Canadian government have always placed tremendous importance on our relationship with the United States. After all, they are the only neighbour with whom we share a border. Former Canadian prime minister Pierre Trudel used the analogy of an elephant and a mouse in describing the relationship between the two nations while speaking to the Washington Press Club in 1971.

"While the United States does not have to be overly concerned about the Canadian mouse, the mouse—no matter how friendly and even-tempered the elephant—must be affected by its every twitch and grunt."

CHAPTER 1.

We Play the Cards We Are Dealt

Dustin Trudel was one of the youngest national leaders in the world. He was elected Canada's prime minister in October 2015. According to *People, Us, Star* and countless other tabloids and talk shows, he was also one of the sexiest men alive. Much to his chagrin, his young wife Sophia bought and kept a copy of each of those magazines. The latest magazine was *Cosmo*, whose cover had a picture of her shirtless husband training for a boxing match. Sophia was giggling as she showed Dustin the cover and put the magazine in a cedar chest with others. "Sophia, I wish you wouldn't…"

"Fame is fleeting, baby. I wanna be able to show my grandchildren and my girlfriends how sexy my husband was in 2016."

As is normal in most democracies, Canadians begin to dislike a new prime minister fifteen to twenty seconds after election, leading to hatred by a large majority of the population a week or two after that. Although Trudel definitely had his detractors, he still had a 54 per cent approval rating thirteen months after his election. The fact that the honeymoon wasn't over yet confounded his critics and delighted his fans and political allies. And the rest of the world outside Canada absolutely adored him and his family.

"Honey, is this a free evening for us, or…? The kids and I haven't seen you in forever."

Dustin glanced up from his briefing notes and sighed. "I'm sorry, *ma cherie*—I'm being picked up in twenty minutes. We have a Cabinet meeting tonight. Part of that meeting will include watching the election in the US as the votes are tabulated. We need to know who is running the show for the next four years."

Sophia was unimpressed. "I could save you all a lot of time. There aren't enough insane people in America to elect an arrogant, impulsive racist pig like Donald Trimp. Therefore, Mallory Clifton wins by default. The polls have her ahead by three per cent. A year ago the polls here had you ahead by four per cent, and you won by a landslide. Do you want to bet on this one?" she teased, hand out, ready to shake.

"No. I don't want to bet on it, because I hope that you are right. But polls often have a margin of error. Besides, even if Mallory Clifton wins, we need to know who's who at the governor and senator level. And at the end of the day, we need to maintain good relations with our American friends no matter who they elect. This is our biggest trading partner, so we need to manage these relations carefully. And don't you forget what the press secretary said about making controversial statements."

Sophia Trudel was an outspoken feminist and former host of an informative morning show in Quebec. Shortly after Trimp won the Republican nomination, Sophia did a live interview in which she roundly ridiculed the Republican candidate, and questioned the depth of the genetic pool of his supporters.

"You mean like calling Donald Trimp a psychotic narcissist? Or an uninformed, dangerous, racist, sexist bully with the maturity level of an 8 year old child? And calling his followers slack-jawed yokels who represent the seamy, greedy hate filled underbelly of America?"

"Yes, I mean like that." Sophia began to laugh. "No, seriously, baby—you can think it, but you can't say it out loud."

"So, a buffoon like Mr. Trimp gets to think out loud and spout whatever dangerous right-wing rhetoric pops into his empty head, but the rest of us have to be politically correct?"

A knock at the living room door saved the prime minister from arguing the point further. "Sir, the car's pulling around now," informed a handler. "Shall I have them wait or…?"

"No. Thanks, Jim—I'm all set. *Bonsoir, ma cherie. Je t'aime.*" Trudel pulled on his coat and kissed his wife goodnight. "Don't wait up. We might be late."

As the American election unfolded on November 8, 2016, the Liberal Cabinet ministers in attendance were riding an emotional roller coaster. Key swing states were hanging in the balance, with races in many ridings too close to call. Hope for a Clifton victory was being gradually replaced by fear, dread and nausea. Around midnight, as the shock of what was happening—*Really? They are voting for The Donald?*—began to set in, the Cabinet ministers, approximately 51 per cent of Americans and 90 per cent of the rational people in the free world were dealing with the first stage of grief: Denial.*

As president-elect Donald Trimp was giving his victory speech, Dustin Trudel surveyed his Cabinet. His ministers looked shattered, shell-shocked, talking to each other in hushed tones. He sat up in his chair and cleared his throat to get their attention.

"Well, I think we can all agree that this is not the outcome we were expecting. Personally—just among us—I am shocked and disappointed. But that is not what we are going to tell the public. Going forward, this is our message to the people."

He stood up to ensure he had everyone's full attention. "The American people have made a democratic choice for president. We support their choice, and look forward to a peaceful transition of power, and working with the Trimp administration. Full stop. Don't ad lib anything else. Don't add your own thoughts. Jim just sent every member of our party those exact words by e-mail. Questions?"

The PM waited a few seconds. "Let's reconvene at ten a.m. tomorrow. I want us to have a roundtable about ways to best work with this new administration. Thanks and good night."

---

*There are five stages of grief: denial, anger, bargaining, depression and acceptance.

The ride back to the PM's residence at 24 Sussex was pretty quiet.

"Sir, is there anything I can do to help you out before tomorrow morning?" Jim MacAuley was, a workhorse—*Maybe even a cyborg?*—and an extremely resourceful executive assistant.

"Umm, sure. Could you make me a list of senators and governors by state? Some of those names might still be in flux. Also, I'm gonna need Mr. Trimp's number. I'll call him at noon our time from my office to congratulate him on his election. And we'll leave here at nine-thirty tomorrow."

"Indeed, sir. Just call me if you think of anything else between now and nine-thirty." Jim opened the back door of the limo. The RCMP driver saluted smartly as the prime minister exited the car.

"Good night, Jim. Good night, Corporal LaFontaine. Thank you both."

Sophia Trudel was still up, watching post-election results in a small TV room off the formal living room. It was obvious she had been crying, and she looked pale and sick.

"Baby, are you all right?" That didn't help, as Sophia began to cry again. While Dustin Trudel held his wife, she got a lot of emotion off her chest.

"Is this even real? I mean, is it a mistake? How could people vote for this monster, this con man, this, this hideous pig? The Oobimas and Cliftons must be just shattered."

Eventually, she stopped sobbing, and they just held each other for a few minutes.

"Mommy, I just had a bad dream." Eugenie was their youngest child. The Trudels had fallen asleep on the couch.

Us too, Genie, thought the PM. *Us, too.* As Sophia consoled the girl and began to take her back to bed, Prime Minister Trudel flicked off the TV. Fox News was playing Trimp's acceptance speech again.

CHAPTER 2.

Political Science 101

Benjamin Big Canoe was a really good teacher. At least his students thought so, especially the girls. Maybe it was an inherited skill. Benjamin's father, Laurent, was a hockey player from an Algonquin Reserve in northern Ontario. When he met Benjamin's mother, Suzanne, she was a rich hippie chick-slash-anthropology major at the University of Nevada in Las Vegas.

Benjamin's parents met after a hockey game in which Laurent had played well, scoring a goal and, more importantly to the fans in attendance, nearly beating an opposing player to death on the ice with his bare hands. Suzanne and her friends had never been to a hockey game, but she never forgot that first one.

"It's so primal," she told her friends. Suzanne and Laurent Big Canoe met at a private party hosted by the team owner in his casino after the game. They were united in holy matrimony—after quite a few rails of Peruvian

Pink Flake—by an Elvis impersonator at four o'clock that morning.

The story of their marriage was well known, in part because they were still together and loved each other after thirty years, and in part because they were always being asked how they had met. The *'love at first sight after hockey game, cocaine fuelled, Elvis impersonator wedding'* was a great story after all. Apparently, not many of those weddings stand the test of time.

Suzanne eventually taught anthropology at the University of Toronto. After Laurent retired from hockey, he also became a teacher of sorts. Laurent loved to hunt and fish, so he started a very successful camp for young people in trouble with addictions or the law or both. He and his counsellors took these young folks to Northern Ontario for a month (after the parents or the province had signed the waivers and paid in full, of course). They went in by float plane with minimal supplies, and essentially lived off the land. Laurent and the other counsellors had pretty good success with their charges once they were dried out and realized that the closest WiFi or cellphone connection was 400 miles southeast.

His lesson plan was simple: "respect yourself, respect each other, respect the land."

Benjamin Big Canoe was the eldest of Laurent and Suzanne's children. He had worked with his dad as a counsellor at the camp for a few summers while studying political science. Maybe that gave him the teaching bug. He did his undergrad at the University of British Columbia, and subsequently completed his master's degree at the University of Toronto. While there, he got to witness how much his mother enjoyed teaching. He was almost finished his doctorate when St. Mary's University in Halifax hired him to be an assistant professor in their political science department.

"So, that's my story," he told his class, wrapping up his introduction. He wasn't going to go there, but several of the bolder girls in the front row got him started with the "Where is Dr. MacAllister, who are you and where are you from?" line of questions.

You know, the kinds of questions all popular perky girls ask of cute male substitute teachers to avoid learning or studying whatever that particular sub is in to teach. "I'll get to know more about each of you as time permits."

"This is Political Science 101, right? Good. So I'm in the right room at least. "His students laughed on cue. "I want to start today with a discussion about what's happening right here, right now. Who is currently our prime minister, and how did he get that job?"

Over the next eighty-five minutes, Benjamin and the forty-eight students in Poli Sci 101 discussed the current state of Canadian politics. Benjamin was pretty good at getting his students to talk. Here is some of that discussion.

"Dustin Trudel is Canada's current prime minister," stated a girl in a hijab.

"When did he get the job?" asked Benjamin.

"Well, as the leader of the Liberal Party of Canada, he was elected as the prime minister in October 2015" the Muslim girl stated. "Apparently tired of scandals, Canadians threw out the ruling Conservative party led by Stephen Sharpe and gave Mr. Trudel's Liberal Party a majority government.

"Minority or Majority? Which is better for the people?" asked Benjamin.

"A Canadian prime minister with a majority government has the opportunity to exercise significant executive and legislative power," said a quiet guy in the back row who had clearly opened the textbook at some point.

"So all right-leaning Canadians who hadn't voted Liberal feared the worst," added the emo girl beside him.

"Why? What are people afraid of?"

"People were sayin' crazy things," Emo Girl continued, "like the Liberals will tax and spend us into bankruptcy on social programs."

"Increased social programs, more government, more welfare," added a very pretty black girl with a banging Afro.

"At least in a minority government," the class heard, "there are checks and balances that ensure the government of the day can't accomplish anything too radical—Liberals can't lean too far left, Conservatives can't lean too far right, etcetera."

"So, is it fair to say that a minority government is a tremendously Canadian way of ensuring that nothing too radical or effective is ever allowed to happen?" Benjamin wondered aloud. "Even if something radical or effective should happen to be required?"

That got the class buzzing. "Wait, wait—back up, one at a time," Benjamin said, hands raised. "First, tell me how many seats I need to win to form government in Canada."

"In Canada, the political party that wins the most seats, ridings or electoral districts traditionally forms the government, and the leader of that party becomes the prime minister. If a party wins more than half of the three hundred and thirty-eight seats—one hundred and seventy—it forms what we call a majority government. So, in Canadian history it has always been either the Liberal or Conservative party who formed the government. For example, if the Liberals got elected, the Conservative Party usually formed the official Opposition, and vice-versa. It's not uncommon to form a majority government in Canada despite the fact there are more than just two federal parties. Especially in recent history," explained one of the front-row girls.

Smart and perky, Benjamin noted. "Talk to me about these other parties."

"Well, sir," began a skinny black student in colourful robes, "there is a federal party that represents only the interest of the mainly French-speaking province of Quebec. The Bloc Québécois' supposed or theoretical main goal is to eventually have La Belle Province separate from Canada and become their own country. Nudge, nudge, wink, wink—they don't really mean it," he said in a funny stage voice.

"They really exist just to ensure that Quebec gets a great deal no matter what legislation, law or act is being discussed. The Bloc knows that they will never form government."

"Are they really a federal party?" Benjamin asked, pretending to be surprised.

"He's not kidding, sir" added one of the front-row girls. "You just can't make this stuff up. But most Canadians don't believe that Quebec will ever separate."

"There's always hope," cracked a kid dressed in jeans complete with Western boots, big belt buckle and a

Stetson. "Quebeckers have used the threat of separation very successfully over the years to make sure their voices were heard. If you discuss the separation issue in Alberta where I'm from, most people would ask, 'What can I do to speed up that process?' or 'What's taking them so long? They've been threatening to separate for fifty years. Man up Quebec—pull the trigger and go already.'"

"Well- you have a point regarding how smartly Quebec has used the threat of separation over the years. Just a heads up for you though: half of this years football team is from Quebec, so lets tread lightly on that topic. "All right. We were discussing other political parties in Canada, and why it's difficult to form a majority government in this country. Who's next? Someone other than these girls in the front row. C'mon, talk to me, talk to us," he encouraged, pacing from left to right at the front of the small theatre.

"The New Democratic Party?" volunteered a shy Korean girl.

"What do they stand for?" prodded Benjamin.

"They are kind of like Liberals, but slightly farther left in the political spectrum," she speculated. "Or at least that is what people seem to think. Nobody in Canada seems really sure what the NDP would do if put in power over the country. But they are riding a recent wave of popularity, due mostly to some questionable leadership choices by the Liberals and Bloc Quebecois, and after the federal election in 2011, the NDP were surprised to wake up as the official Opposition to the Conservative party. It was the first time in Canadian history that a party other than the Liberals or Conservatives had formed the Official opposition."

"Well said. Thank you. You mentioned a political spectrum. Let's talk about that for a few minutes," Benjamin said, heading for the whiteboard at the front of the class. He glanced at his watch, and switched into lecture mode. As a professor, he enjoyed class participation, but he also needed to ensure that his points of view were heard; he would eventually need to test them on something he or the textbook had taught them.

"Of course, Canada allows pretty much anyone that is of legal age and a Canadian citizen to run for government. There is a Green Party, a Marxist-Leninist Party, a Christian Heritage Party, a Rhinoceros Party, a Social Credit Party, a Marijuana Party—" Benjamin raised his hands here to quell the chuckles and chatter "—and if they ever form a government, we should all open a pizza shop, because business will be booming. Okay, okay, calm down. There are more parties, but you get the picture. Few of these parties have actually seen any of their members be elected, but they certainly liven up the local debates. And you need not be tied to a political party to run for political office, Canadians are free to run for office as independents as well."

Benjamin drew a long line on the board, with a left, a right and a *C* in the middle.

Left	Centre	Right

"A political spectrum. Let's put some of these parties on the spectrum. What party would be farthest left?

"The NDP?' asked the cowboy hopefully.

The Mouse Who Poked an Elephant ∗ 23

"Well, yes, in practical terms, if we are doing the spectrum just for those parties who have current elected members of Parliament, you are correct. For now, let's put the NDP in between left and centre. But what political ideology is far, far left of the NDP?"

"Communism," volunteered the Korean girl quietly.

"Indeed. Now going from left to right, what parties or ideologies fill out this spectrum? Let's include our American and British friends, as well. You shout it, I'll write it. It may add a point of reference for us in further discussion."

Within the next few minutes, here is what the class arrived at.

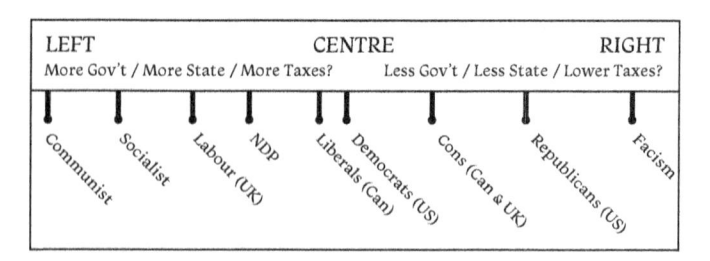

LEFT	CENTRE	RIGHT
More Gov't / More State / More Taxes?		Less Gov't / Less State / Lower Taxes?

Communist — Socialist — Labour (UK) — NDP — Liberals (Can) — Democrats (US) — Cons (Can & UK) — Republicans (US) — Facism

"Sir, on the spectrum, shouldn't Mr. Trimp's Republicans be farther right than fascism?" asked one of the front-row girls. That got the crowd hooting.

"OK, calm down. The man has barely started his new and rather demanding job. In the interest of fairness, we can better assess his leadership after he has had a chance to lead. Let's give him a year in the job before we criticize him or his party.

"Now, back on to our topic—this political spectrum— we are close enough." Benjamin continued, turning back to the class. "Some party purists might argue we are off a degree or two, but that's good for now. As you can see, in Canada, the two parties that have traditionally held power are pretty close to the centre.

"So, now you can see why it's difficult for any party in Canada to form a majority. Canadians have a lot of choice when voting in an election. Only four political parties had a representative running in all three hundred and thirty-eight electoral districts in the last election: the Conservative Party, the Liberal Party, the New Democratic Party and the Green Party. The Bloc Quebecois only runs for election in the seventy-five Quebec seats, the Western Alliance only runs for election in Western Canada, and so on.

"Given all of these choices, a typical result after a Canadian election would be a minority government. For example in 2006," Benjamin went on, turning again to the whiteboard, "the Conservatives won one hundred and twenty-four seats, the Liberals one hundred and three, the Bloc Quebecois fifty-one, the NDP twenty-nine, and there was one Independent."

"Show of hands, please. How many people consider themselves to be on the left side of the political spectrum?" A large majority of the students raised their hands. "Look around. It looks like eighty to eighty-five per cent of us in this room favour parties on the left. So how did a party on the right, the Conservatives, win a majority in 2011?

"Maybe we don't accurately reflect who voted," the pretty black girl with the seventies' Afro suggested. Now Benjamin recognized the speaker from a photo in the school paper. She had just been elected as the

The Mouse Who Poked an Elephant * 25

president of the university's student council. Her name was Juliette Sparks.

"Explain, please."

"Well, Elijah did several rants on low voter turnout among young people. So we may think we are on the left, but if we don't actually vote…"

"Mmm…you may be on to something there," Benjamin mused. "I like a lot of what Elijah says, and in his recent rant regarding young voters, he's quoting statistics from Elections Canada. However, voter turnout, especially among your demographic—" he gestured at the students with a sweeping motion "—increased significantly in the most recent federal election. So I'm confused."

"Wait, you're the professor. If you're confused, imagine how we feel," chirped one of the front-row girls wearing a short plaid schoolgirl skirt, to general laughter. Benjamin laughed along with his class, but it was getting harder to stay on topic.

"Okay, I'll ask the question a different way," said Benjamin, moving back behind the podium. Do you think your parents and grandparents used to lean left politically, and gradually turned to the right?"

"Maybe we are idealists in our youth, and become more realistic as we get older," offered Emo Girl.

"Where are you going with that?"

"I think the answer is on the top of our political spectrum chart," she went on. "The chart indicates that the farther left we lean, the more government involvement we have in the state. That means more social programs, welfare, free healthcare, free daycare, old-age pensions, free education…"

"Wait, that stuff all sounds expensive," interjected Benjamin. "How can it be free?"

"It's not free. The money comes from taxes. As a young person, all those programs sound like a great idea, but young people don't earn a lot of money and therefore don't pay a lot of taxes."

Clever girl, thought Benjamin. *Now we are getting to the nuts and bolts of it.*

"Then, as we get older, and hopefully get jobs, we will start to pay more tax, and eventually start to resent all those tax-funded programs."

"Why would we resent social programs?" prodded Benjamin. "Aren't these programs good for all of us?"

"People resent paying for programs that they likely won't ever use themselves," suggested rodeo boy.

"Such as?"

"Well, like welfare or employment insurance. Out west, until recently, we have had low unemployment. So, a large majority of people out there were working and paying taxes to fund welfare and EI, but very few people out west ever used those programs. So they began to resent the people who collected those benefits on a regular basis."

"Whoa, pardner. So you're sayin' all east-coasters are lazy bums on welfare?" bristled a kid with a Cape Breton Island T-shirt.

This is getting interesting, Benjamin thought. *Or weird and dangerous.*

"Actually, no. I'm quoting east-coasters who are working in the oil patch. My family is from Springhill, dude, just a ways up the road, but my dad moved us out west twenty years ago when the coal mines closed. If there's no work, people should move to where the work is." The speaker seemed reluctant to have a class half full of Maritimers hating on him. "Look, I'm not trying to pick a fight here. I'm just saying that most people resent paying tax for programs that they won't get a return on."

"So do Canadians vote differently based on where we live or how much we earn?" asked Benjamin.

There was an awkward pause. "Well, yes. I mean, I'm not from here, and I can't vote, so I don't know if…" the black kid in tribal dress seemed reluctant to go any further.

"Go ahead," Benjamin encouraged. "You don't need to be a Canadian to comment on a political system. Forgive my curiosity. Where are you from, anyway?"

"Côte D'Ivoire, sir."

"Good. Listen, to put the shoes on other feet, we're discussing emerging African nations next week, and I'll expect everyone else to participate in that discussion. Regional voting preferences. You were saying?"

"Sir, the latest electoral map of Canada on page one-sixty-three—" he paused as his fellow students grabbed the textbook and flipped through pages to see what he was referring to "—in our text shows a clear regional voting preference. In simple terms, the map of the east coast is a pure Liberal red. There is a bit of each party elected in Quebec. Ontario voted primarily for the Liberal Party. But from Manitoba west, the map is very blue, except for urban ridings in British Columbia. From this, it appears that Western Canadians prefer the Conservative ideology—less government interference and fewer social programs eventually resulting in lower taxes. The same voter preferences can be seen to some extent in the United States, where urban voters on both coasts generally vote for the Democratic party and the voters in the heartland, rural areas and rustbelts prefer the Republican party."

"Okay, good observations, thank you. So if we draw a line at the border of Ontario and Manitoba, the country seems politically divided between east and west. Why did that happen?"

"There's more young people working out west in private enterprise," offered up the cowboy.

"But I thought we said young people generally prefer the left of the spectrum," Benjamin countered.

"Maybe we do, until we start paying taxes, then lower taxes seem like a pretty good idea," rebutted the cowboy.

"So now you're sayin' everyone east of Quebec is old, lazy or on welfare and that's why we vote Liberal and NDP?" said the kid in the Cape Breton shirt. He looked ready to jump out of his seat.

"No, I'm not saying that at all, but the map seems to say it"

"Oooooooh," and "Oh, no, you didn't!" yelled a few in the crowd.

"Okay, okay, everybody calm down," Benjamin urged. "This isn't Jerry Stringer. I don't have security to clean this up if it gets messy. But it's cool that we are having a political discussion with some emotion. We have been discussing majority versus minority governments and the political spectrums on a left to right scale. I am going to suggest that it should be simple for one party to stay in power with majority governments consistently, given the current political spectrum."

The class looked confused. "Did Dr MacAllister have you read chapter three in the text?" *You were supposed to—it was in MacAllister's notes.* Heads were nodding in affirmation throughout the room.

"Chapter three was about the political spectrum—not just here in Canada, but all over the world. Does anyone remember what the author said about the percentage of left-right preferences in established democracies?"

"She had graphs for the USA, the UK, Australia and Canada," offered Quiet Back-Row Guy. "In each country, the preference between left and right was close, like, fifty-one per cent lefties versus forty-nine per cent righties." Emo girl passed him her text. "Oh, thanks. Yeah—page seventy-two, four graphs over the past twenty years—people's preferences between left and right are close in all four similar democracies."

"If that is the case, then one party in Canada should be able to win elections just by where they sit on the political spectrum, no?" Professor Big Canoe continued.

"Sure," said Emo Girl. "There's three or four main parties on the left, and only one on the right. So in theory, in almost every electoral district, if roughly fifty per cent of the population votes left, those votes will get split between the Liberal, NDP, Greens or the Bloc, si vous habitez au Quebec. Meanwhile, the other fifty per cent of society who lean to the political right are mostly all voting Conservative. So," she concluded, "we might have been stuck with Stephen Sharpe for our prime minister until the end of time."

"So," Benjamin pressed on, "how did Stephen Sharpe lose the last election? He had a majority government, and according to what we just discussed, he and his party should have won the last election thanks to the division of votes by all the left-of-centre parties. What happened to him and his party?"

"The Senate scandal," several students offered.

"Robocalls" said another.

"His fishin' buddy, Big Ron Forde, didn't help his image any," suggested the Cape Breton kid, which got a lot of laughs.

"'Cause Dustin Trudel is a smoke show," chimed in two of the front-row girls, resulting in chaotic laughter and screams.

"Alright, everybody calm down," Benjamin requested. "Nobody becomes prime minister simply by being incredibly good looking."

"But it didn't hurt our current prime minister's chances," chirped back the girls, to more general laughter from the whole class.

"All right, all right, we have two minutes left. Come on, in general terms—notwithstanding the cuteness factor—how did a party that seemed destined to win more elections lose like the Conservatives did in 2015?"

"They stayed too long in power," said Juliette Sparks quietly.

"What do you mean by that?" asked Benjamin.

"It's a natural progression, especially in politics," the girl explained. "When people first start in a job, they make decisions tentatively, almost by committee, asking their staff, 'Am I able to do this or buy that?' They don't want to overstep their authority. But after three or five years or ten years in the chair, they get more confident, and start telling people how it's going to work, rather than asking them. And then they get cocky and overstep their legal authority, or just make mistakes. Look at Margaret Thackeray's government in the UK, or Brian Muldoon, or…"

"Or the bunga-bunga guy in Italy," added one of the front-row girls.

"Jacques Chretien and Donald Regan," suggested the cowboy.

"Okay, okay." Benjamin made a chopping motion across his throat. "So it seems there's a trend? If a person or party stays too long in power, what's the general theme?"

"They start to mess up, and we throw them out," said the Cape Bretoner.

"We don't elect new governments, we just throw the old ones out," quoted Juliette.

"Yes. I like that statement." *There's only a minute left.* "So, is our political system—this constitutional monarchy—broken beyond repair? If it is broken, how do we fix it?"

Several students raised their hands, eager to answer but Benjamin waved them off. "Rather than discuss it, I want a five thousand-word essay explaining your plans to improve our country's current political system. It's due to Professor MacAllister by e-mail two weeks from today, no later than midnight."

The class groaned in unison, as if they were one massive team of galley slaves chained to their oars who had just been informed that the captain wished to waterski.

"This afternoon I will send out the detailed parameters of what I'm looking for in the paper to your e-mail addresses we have on file. Questions?"

"Sir, may we speak with you after class? asked the blonde girl in the front row.

"Of course, I'll stay behind." *But I'm already nervous,* thought Benjamin. "Any other questions?"

There weren't. The class was already emptying out, and the four very cute girls from the front row were closing in on Benjamin like wolves on a wounded deer.

"Yes, ladies—you had a question?" Benjamin asked. *Good heavens, I'm as nervous as a fifteen-year-old Amish kid on his wedding night. Calm down, they're the students…you're the professor.*

"Yes, we do have a question," began their spokesperson. "We're having a keg party this Friday night in our residence, and we would love it if you could attend."

"I'm sorry, I…I just can't do that. My mother is a teacher, and when I accepted this job, I asked if she had any advice for me. She said yes—don't become friends with your students, and don't go to keg parties in dorms."

"Aww, it's just adorable that you still listen to your mom." The other girls nodded cheerfully in agreement, making those noises that girls make when they see a wagon full of ducklings being pulled by a puppy.

Benjamin realized he was blushing and staring at his feet like a four-year-old.

"Well, maybe some other time," the girl breezed on. "If you have any questions about the school, or hot spots downtown, we'd be happy to show you around." And with a hair flip that signaled "We're outta here" to her crew they were gone. Benjamin breathed a sigh of relief.

When he got back to the office, there were two voicemails on his phone. The first was from Dr. MacAllister, Benjamin's sponsor and mentor.

"Hey, Ben. I forgot to warn you. You're a young teacher. Students like young teachers, so…um… some of the students may want to become friendly with you. Now that I'm saying this, I feel stupid. Anyway. Just be careful. We'll talk next week when I get back from the conference. You have my cell number should we need to talk prior to that."

The second message was from his friend Elijah. "Hey, Ben—congrats on the new teaching gig. I love the paper you sent me. A lot of good ideas. Let me know when you want to start. Later, brother. Love, peace and chicken grease."

CHAPTER 3.

Maybe Chicken Little Was Right...

"The Group of Twenty, or G20 will hold an emergency summit in Berlin beginning this Friday to discuss strategies to resuscitate the free-falling global econ—"

Click.

"This is CNN News. In our lead story, the Dow Jones continued to free fall today, losing another six per cent of its value. The Dow Jones Industrial Average has plummeted from a record high of 20,200 in December 2016, and closed trading today at 13,403 points. Our guest today is the Chairman of the United States Federal Reserve—"

Click.

"All major stock markets closed sharply down today, with the Nikkei and Shanghai Composite posting the worst loss."

Click.

"…Cash money for your gold jewelry. We pay top—"

Click.

"…The G20 economies control eighty-six per cent of the GWT or gross world tra—"

Click.

"Prepare to pay more at the pumps. Gas prices in Ontario jumped eleven cents today, with provincial regulators predicting that further increases are likely."

Click.

"This week on *The Kardoshians*, Cami and Clooey go wild in New Yor—"

"Ah, finally. Something that's not bad news." Estelle Trudel had invited two of the coolest girls from her school for a sleepover. It hadn't been much fun so far. Her friends were cool, but all the parental units in the world were freaking out lately.

"Oh. My. God. Look. at. what. Cami's. wearing," giggled one of her friends.

"I know, it makes her look so fa—"

"We interrupt our regularly scheduled programming to bring you this important message from the president of the United States of America."

"Muuuuuuuuum—there's nothing on TV but bad news!" Estelle was yelling to her mother in the kichen. *Tell me something I don't know, kiddo,* Sophia thought, walking to the TV room.

"That's because there are a lot of things changing in the world right now. honey" Sophia told Estelle. *And most people don't react well to change.* "Why don't you three go for a walk, or play a board game or do some homework?"

Estelle sighed, shooting her friends a look of exasperation intended to mean: *My Mom is such a dweeb.* "A—it's freezing rain out. B—Board games are, well, boring, and C—only nerds do homework at sleepovers."

"*Ma cherie*, can I speak with you for a moment please," Sophia's husband called from his office in the library. There were two efficient-looking men in the office with the prime minister. Both were speaking on cell phones when Sophia entered. "Honey, I'm sorry, the timing has been advanced for the Berlin summit. We're flying out of Ottawa within the hour."

"Will you be back in time for our anniversary this Sunday? Or had you forgotten?" Sophia teased.

"No, I hadn't forgotten. I'm sorry, honey, it looks right now like the summit may go on until at least Tuesday."

He looks so tired, Sophia was thinking. This last couple of years had taken its toll on her husband. *What a shitty job. Why does anyone sign up for this level of abuse?* "Is there anything I can do to help you over the next few days, Mr. Prime Minister?" Sophia asked her husband, brushing some lint off his shoulder.

"Just try to stay positive for the kids…and everybody else. The news lately has been hard to take. Oh, and could you review the menu for the Japanese president's dinner we're hosting next week? Mme D'Entremont at Rideau Hall has all the details." The PM's aides were waiting by the office door.

"Japanese president's dinner menu. Got it. Call when you can, let me know when you're coming home."

"I will. Estelle, be good for your mom," Dustin said, giving her a quick kiss. "Girls, enjoy your sleepover."

The Mouse Who Poked an Elephant ⋆ 37

"I will, and we will, Popsicle. Are you going somewhere?"

"Yes, honey, I have to go to Berlin for a meeting. Your mom can explain more, I've gotta fly." He held his arms out as if he were actually flying. *No? Nothing? Tough audience ...*

One aide was holding the front door open expectantly, and Dustin Trudel could see the limo idling outside, with an RCMP officer waiting at attention. As the prime minister stepped outside, the Mountie opened the car door and saluted smartly. A few seconds later, the car disappeared into the mist.

"Hey, Estelle, look, your dad's on TV again," one of her friends was saying. Well, it wasn't actually Mr. Trudel on the screen. It was an effigy of the prime minister—a set of coveralls stuffed with straw—on the great lawn in front of the Parliament Buildings wearing a Dustin Trudel mask. It looked harmless at first. Until a protestor tied a noose around the effigy's neck and lit the effigy on fire.

"I think that's enough TV for now, ladies," Sophia stated, hitting the off button on the remote. "Estelle, why don't you show the girls the pool? I think your brother is just going for a swim now," she said, nodding at the closed-circuit TV that showed Xanadu Trudel and the French ambassador's son diving into the pool.

"That's a great idea, Mrs Trudel," said Estelle's friend Britney. "Can we change in your room, Estelle?" asked Emily. Estelle sighed.

"Sure, c'mon, let's go." *My big brother is such a dweeb,* she was thinking. But she knew that Britney and Emily thought otherwise. *Gross.*

The next five days passed almost normally for Sophia and her family. Well, as normally as could be expected for the wife and children of an elected leader in 2017. Unfortunately, the same could not be said for the leaders and economic ministers of the G20 nations in Berlin.

The Group of Twenty is comprised of the twenty largest economies in the world. Collectively, these member countries account for 86 per cent of gross world trade, and 66 per cent of the world's population. The smaller economies in the European Union—Ireland, Portugal, Greece, etc.— are represented by the president of the European Council together as one voting member. Critics of the G20 love to point out that it is essentially an elitist club for world leaders who have enough money to buy a membership. Other critics compare it to a high school, where there is usually a clique of the twenty coolest kids. If you don't think, dress, walk, text and talk like the cool kids, you can never hope to be in the cool kid club. No big money? Not cool? No membership.

So at any given time, approximately 170 countries in the world are not invited to the party. Of all the African nations, only South Africa has a large enough economy to sit at the G20 table. Similarly, Brazil and Argentina are the only two South American countries invited to the dance. Most non-member nations are poor when compared by GDP to member nations.

"And most non member nations are populated by persons of colour," G20 denouncers are fond of adding. There are some exceptions of course. For example, the Scandinavian countries are very well-developed, and have some of the highest standards of living in the world. But their economies aren't big enough by themselves to merit inclusion in the G20, and they are not members of the European Union.

Norway's foreign minister, Jonas Gahr Støre, called the G20 "One of the greatest global setbacks since World War Two. The G20 is a self-appointed group. Its composition is determined by the major countries and powers. It may be more representative than the G7 or the G8, in which only the richest countries are represented, but it is still arbitrary. We no longer live in the nineteenth century, a time when the major powers met and redrew the map of the world. No one needs a new Congress of Vienna."

Critics of the G20 are visibly and audibly noticeable whenever and wherever the G20 chooses to meet annually. If you think back to any scenes in which police in riot gear were required for crowd control, you are likely remembering scenes from a recent G20 summit.

During his flight from Ottawa to Berlin, Prime Minister Trudel studied a briefing of the latest financial numbers from the various G20 nations that his staff had prepared. *None of these numbers paint a pretty picture,* he thought. *Maybe now Canadians will appreciate how well off we are in comparison to other G20 nations.*

Canada's economy had weathered the recession in 2008 to 2013 fairly well. (Again, at least, when compared to their G20 counterparts.) The Conservatives had high-lighted Stephen Sharpe's tough leadership style and experience as an economist as the reasons for the country's (relatively) healthy economy from 2008 forward until 2015. *It could be worse,* the prime minister thought to himself as he closed the dossier. *It could have been our turn to host and chair the summit.*

You didn't need to be an economist to know that most of the major economies in the world were in very bad shape. Major stock market indexes all over the world were down significantly. Unemployment figures had nearly doubled in the USA, Canada, the UK and the larger European nations. Brazil, Mexico, South Africa and some of the smaller European nations were dealing with 20 to 30 per cent unemployment numbers. Each of the G20 nations were paying interest on record high levels of debt. And in many of the G20 countries, average individual citizens were carrying more personal debt than ever before.

To make matters more difficult for any person, enterprise or government who was in debt, interest rates were climbing quickly: from a historically long period with rates below 4 per cent, back into the 8 per cent range, with predictions that rates might rise as high as 15 percent. This recent rise in interest rates was resulting in a massive upswing in real estate listings and bankruptcies. In most major cities, homes were for sale at 1990s prices. Supply was overwhelming, but no one was buying for fear that a greater economic downturn was yet to come.

A lot of people blamed President Donald Trimp and the United States for their recent economic difficulties. Shortly after being sworn in, Trimp led the USA down a very protectionist path. In the interest of protecting American jobs, he began to tax imports. Of course this was in direct violation of most free trade agreements, but, he was backed up by the world's mightiest military, complete with enough nuclear weapons to destroy the world one hundred times over. The world - in a nutshell - viewed Trimp as a loudmouth bully with a huge military. Of even greater concern was the fact that he seemed willing to deploy this military force at the slightest provocation.

In every G20 nation, inflation had also reared its head again in the past twelve months. Not the 2 per cent inflation that most people—including economists and bankers (who lots of people believed weren't people at all)—had become comfortable with in the first thirteen years of the new century.

No, sir—this was 1980s-style "kick you right in the nuts" inflation, which had driven the cost of most household goods - fuel, food, electricity, clothing, etc- up at least 15 per cent over the past twelve months. To make matters even worse, those countries who had printed record amounts of extra money to prop up their economies, stock markets and banks (like the good old US of A), now found that the value of their dollar was diminishing rapidly.

The world leaders managed to paste on stoic smiles during the photo shoot at the reception and dinner of the first evening at the emergency summit in Berlin. But there was little smiling after the photo. The president of the European Council, Herman von Rumpey, was chairing this summit. An American journalist once mistakenly referred to him as Herman the German. The mistake became legend when a female Belgian reporter pointed out the error to the journalist from Dallas on live TV.

"You mean to say Belgium isn't part of Germany?" he asked.

"No. We are a separate and independent nation," responded the young lady indignantly.

"Well, then," drawled the Texan, "you fellers should say thanks to my grandfather, 'cause if it wasn't for him and some of his friends, y'all woulda been Germans since 1940." It was a pretty big story in Texas and Brussels for a few weeks. Notwithstanding his infamously mistaken nationality, Mr. von Rumpcy had excellent intentions of keeping the meeting focused and on point, but it was always going to be a very difficult meeting to chair.

The G20 meetings always had a theme. The theme for 2006 was "Building and Sustaining Prosperity." After the world's stock markets staggered and fell to their knees in 2008, the theme was "A Leaders' Summit on Financial Markets and the World Economy." The chairman's first challenge would be trying to get the participants to agree on the theme for this meeting.

"Ladies and Gentlemen. I will ask that we take our seats, and begin what we hope will be a galvanizing point for the days ahead," began Herman von Rumpey. "First, allow me to thank you for arranging your attendance to this summit on regrettably short notice. I believe that time is a precious commodity, and therefore in the interest of efficiency I will request that we begin. I propose that our first point of business be choosing a theme for this summit. I therefore motion that the theme of this summit be 'A Leadership Summit on Stabilizing World Markets.'" Von Rumpey made the Dr. Evil quotation marks with his fingers as he uttered the proposed theme. "The floor is open for discussion from the delegates."

The assembled teams of five or six delegates from each country conferred quickly in hushed tones.

"The chair recognizes the president of the United States of America."

Most eyebrows in the room raised, and hair began to stand up on the back of numerous necks.

To say that Donald Trimp was neither liked nor respected by multitudes worldwide was a massive understatement. As a businessman and reality TV personality he had always been easy to dislike, but he was never considered dangerous.

However, since becoming the president of the United States, he was consistently put in the metaphorical "crazy and dangerous" basket alongside Hitler, Stalin and Satan. And many of those comparisons were from his fellow Americans.

The rest of the world was still struggling to understand how a country as (supposedly) advanced as the USA managed to elect such a dangerously uninformed and arrogant buffoon.

"The Donald" himself, however, seemed oblivious to the fact that apart from recently reemployed coal miners in Appalachia and zealously religious right-wing evangelical 60 round magazine automatic fire assault rifle owners he was loathed, both at home and abroad.

"Thank you, Mr. Chairman," began Donald Trimp. "I'm concerned that the proposed theme title will cause undue panic, leading to further economic decline in many cases. I've got a better theme title."

He was cut off abruptly by the Turkish minister of finance. "If recent economic figures in your country are not reason to panic, you must be mad."

"Order, order," the chairman was bellowing, while banging a gavel. "The president of the United States of America has the floor."

Zhao Xiaochuan outshouted the chair. "The United States, led by this mongrel fool, has been breaking every known free trade agreement in order to protect his own greedy interests. This man and the morally corrupt Americans have brought us all to the point of ruin," shouted the governor of the Chinese central bank.

That got about twenty different delegates shouting at each other all at once. It seemed that the majority of delegates were barking mad at the USA for their hard-line tactics regarding free trade agreements. But there were other problems in addition to the general dislike of President Trimp.

European delegates from the smaller EU nations were screaming that Britain and Germany had abandoned or betrayed Europe.

The Saudi minister of finance had removed a shoe, and was banging it on a table while shrieking that the entire group was" aligned against Muslims."

The South African president, meanwhile, insisted that the G20 was "an oppressor of all African persons, on a greater scale than slavery."

No one was listening to the chair's request for order. He turned, and spoke to an aide seated behind him on the stage. The aide nodded and quickly left the stage.

Suddenly, the room went dark. And silent. After a pause, Herman von Rumpey began to speak. "Gentlemen… and ladies. It is pointless to shout accusations at each other. If we cannot restore order amongst ourselves, what hope do we offer our citizens?"

"In a moment, I'd like to turn the lights back on, with hope that we can conduct our summit in an orderly fashion." He paused again to clear his throat. And waited for what seemed like an eternally long time. "Wolfgang, please turn on the lights."

The delegates blinked, and looked at the floor, embarrassed. The Australian prime minister handed a shoe to the Saudi delegate as inconspicuously as one can return a shoe in a formal international setting. *Awkward*.

Von Rumpey continued unfazed. "Mr. President—I believe you had the floor. Please finish your thought."

However, the president of the United States was no longer in the room. Please understand that in the first seventy years of his life, Donald Trimp was the CEO of companies he inherited or started. Thus, in boardrooms, people quickly learned to agree with his ideas or be fired.

Since he announced his intent to run for political office, however, he had received more bad press and ridicule than anyone since…well, ever. The last member of President Trimp's security detail was closing the door behind the American delegation just as the lights came back on.

"Trimp Quits G20 Summit" was the lead story on every news channel for the next forty-eight hours . The "G20 Minus One Summit" did it's best to move forward with meetings that fit the summit's theme, but the group didn't accomplish anything meaningful. Every country in the G20 (Or was it now G19?) shared similar economic challenges: staggering and increasingly expensive national debt, rising interest rates, falling stock markets, rising unemployment, a collapsed real estate market, high inflation, crumbling infrastructure, and rapidly rising costs of social programs such as old age and public service pensions, healthcare, welfare and unemployment insurance.

Much of the international coverage from European and Asian journalists placed the blame for the dysfunctional summit squarely on the shoulders of President Trump and the USA. Germany was a secondary scapegoat for European journalists, who expounded that Germany should finance loans to all the EU countries in economic crisis. The Australian, Canadian and British press took a more moderate stance. Several journalists suggested that each country should look inward, and find their own solutions rather than expect the USA to save the world, or Germany to save the European Union.

Protestors in Berlin became more angry and aggressive as the summit sputtered to its conclusion. The protestors all had different concerns. Many Germans wanted the G20 abolished. Still others wanted Germany to walk away from the European Union and the Euro. A Nazi flag or two could be seen almost every day somewhere in the mob, but that usually resulted in a fight, and then a fire as the swastika was burned.

"Why are you so upset?" numerous newspersons asked individuals in the crowd.

"Why should the German people save these other lazy undisciplined goatherders in Europe?" a young lady with a very spiky Mohawk responded to a CNN journalist.

"A Greek, French or Italian person begins to receive their retirement pensions at age fifty-five or sixty, yet I must wait until I am sixty-seven?" an older man angrily

The Mouse Who Poked an Elephant * 47

retorted. "Many European countries have expanded their social programs to a level which they cannot realistically hope to sustain. These countries should not expect the German people to bail them out of trouble if they are unwilling to curb their spending. They must get their own houses in order."

Meanwhile, back in the States, Trimpanzees from Portland Maine to Portland Oregon were in rare patriotic form.

"How dare they insult our president?" Fox News asked.

The summit closed with a whimper, having achieved very little. Many of the group's opponents commented that this was possibly the best G20 summit ever, as it had exposed its futility, lack of legitimacy and uselessness.

Dustin Trudel's flight home was uneventful. He used the flight time to catch up on Canadian and international news. None of it was uplifting.

"Do you ever get tired of it all, Bob?" he quietly asked his finance minister. He pointed to a story in a Toronto paper which highlighted yet another alleged boondoggle by his already besieged political party.

Bob Mornay didn't answer. He obviously did get tired of "it," at least enough to have fallen asleep.

CHAPTER 4.

Hotter Than Hot

Elijah was the superstar host of the insanely popular political show, *Power to the People*. Elijah—like Jesus or Cher, he just used the one name—was a Canadian demographer's wet dream: young, fit, trendy, black, hip, funny, handsome, passionate, thoughtful, eloquent, emotional, bi-sexual, trilingual.... He was often described as "dangerously handsome" by people of both sexes.

He had been a child soldier in Somalia who eventually escaped to Canada. He was raised by a lesbian couple in Vancouver who adopted and raised eight other children. Elijah famously turned down a Rhodes Scholarship in 2007 on his way to completing a master's degree in communications.

Wait. What? "Who turns down a Rhodes Scholarship?" he was often asked.

"Someone who recognizes the scholarship fund as a colonial fortune built on the broken and bloodied backs of African slaves, that's who."

"Well, then why did you apply for the scholarship?"

"Can you think of a better way to draw attention to the issue?"

His talk show, *Power to the People*, was being credited for sparking a rare high level of interest in politics worldwide, especially among young people. It was carried on twenty-seven networks across the globe.

Bono, Benjamin Netanyahu, Russell Brand, Prince Charles, Vladimir Putin, Snoop Dogg, the Pope and Sarah Silverman all agreed on one thing: namely that Elijah was the best young journalist working in the English language right now. Some television hosts were famous for who they had interviewed, but Elijah took greater pride in the list of people whom he refused to interview. If you were vacant, vapid or vacuous, you were not going to be interviewed on *Power to the People*.

He also refused to interview assholes. So, in short, Elijah refused interview requests from:

1. All famous but obviously shallow pop music, TV or movie stars striving for attention (any Kirdoshian, for example)
2. Extreme nut-job political megalomaniacs such as US President Donald Trimp and North Korea's Supreme Leader, Kong Jin On.

Elijah is filmed live in Toronto. It's a tough ticket to get, as there are only 800 seats in the studio.

"Ladies and gentlemen, welcome to *Power to the People*, live with Elijah! We be rollin' in three, two, one…" The crowd, mostly young (and very high) went crazy as Elijah took the stage.

"Hey, calm down you crazy kids. Listen, thanks for watching our show. My guest this evening is the minister of international trade for Canada, the honourable Cynthia Forlund." Some of the crowd applauded, but the boos were louder.

"Thank you for having me as a guest, Elijah- I always enjoy your show."

"Minister, most politicians enjoy our show until they appear as guests, then, mmmmnmmmm, not so much." Laughter, applause. "Anyway- let's get this party started. There are several hundred messy, delicious, scandalous and unpopular topics involving the Liberal Party right now that we could discuss. To be fair, we could say that about any government anywhere, unless you live in North Korea." Badump-bump. Elijah's drummer gave him the obligatory cheesy Vegas drum treatment.

"But I digress. Let's talk about the one main issue that falls within your portfolio as minister of trade. I'd like to start with an abridged version of your mandate letter that Prime Minister Trudel gave you after you were appointed."

"Elijah, I'd like to point out that Prime Minister Trudel was the first Canadian PM in some time to give each Cabinet minister a specific mandate letter, and to publicize those letters. We believe it provides an open and transparent mechanism with which the Canadian people can hold us—their elected officials—accountable."

"Agreed. Props for that." Elijah did a golf clap, but not a lot of people joined in. Elijah held up a copy of the letter. "So, as minister of trade, the letter said that your job is 'to increase Canada's trade and attract job-creating investment to Canada, focusing on expanding trade with large fast-growing markets, including China and India, and deepening our trade links with traditional partners.' You are also to work on strategies to implement the Canada-European Union Comprehensive Economic and Trade Agreement (CETA) and consult on Canada's potential participation in the Trans-Pacific Partnership (TPP)."

"Well, Elijah, I'd like to say that we have made progress on each of these files, but—"

"Oh, no, Minister, just hold your horses now," interjected Elijah. "This isn't the House of Commons where people just get up and shout stuff whenever they want to drown out opposing logic. This is Elijah's house. My house, my rules. Don't worry, I'll give you a chance to speak," he said, patting the minister's knee. The crowd cheered raucously. *Everybody loves seeing people in positions of power put in their place.*

"Minister, I honestly believe that you are indeed working diligently to achieve the goals set out in your mandate letter. That's not the problem. The problem is that the international trade agreements are crippling our economy rather than stimulating it." Elijah looked up from his notes and back into the camera. "Here is what a lot of Canadians are thinking—that these free-trade deals, NAFTA, CETA, TPP, etc., are examples of the free-market fundamentalism that has created a global race to the bottom. The countries willing to work for the lowest wages win the jobs. Free trade agreements put commercial interests for big corporations above all other values.

"Under the umbrella of free trade agreements, big corporations move high-paying jobs to countries with lower wages or lower local wages here by threatening to transfer production abroad. NAFTA has worsened poverty and inequality, diminished social programs, and weakened Canadian sovereignty and democracy.

"Minister, the only true winners in NAFTA—and similar proposed future trade agreements—are big corporations and their shareholders. And now is the perfect time for us to get out of all these free trade deals anyway, cause our biggest trading partner is not playing by the rules of the agreement."

The audience screamed, hooted, hollered and clapped their approval.

"Elijah , I don't agree…"

"Oh, thank heavens for that, or this would have been a boring show," Elijah retorted. "Okay, then please tell our viewers why trade agreements are such a good thing for us."

"With pleasure. So, in order to understand why we need trade agreements, let's start by reviewing our first trade agreement. In 1988, we signed the Canada-US Free Trade Agreement—aka CUFTA. CUFTA started a period of remarkable growth in commerce between our two countries. Under CUFTA, Canadian exports to the U.S. rose by 220 per cent, while imports from the US went up by 160 per cent between 1989 and 1994." The minister paused for a sip of water.

"Then in 1994, we signed NAFTA—the North American Free Trade Agreement—which aligned Mexico, the United States and Canada as trading partners.

Essentially, NAFTA decreased or eliminated tariffs between our countries. The reduction in tariffs and trade restrictions brought about by NAFTA has made it easier for American and Mexicans to purchase goods made in Canada, and vice-versa. Elijah, simply put, NAFTA substantially increased trade between our three countries. The bottom line is that NAFTA enhanced the Gross Domestic Product of all three participating countries every year since 1994.

"So looking forward, the TPP and CETA will do the same as NAFTA did for us. These agreements will open up phenomenal new markets for Canadians. The TPP and CETA can expand our potential customer base from 360 million North American people to over four billion people." The minister leaned forward and smiled. "So, does that help to explain why our government wants to expand our free trading partners to include South America, the Carribbean, Europe and Asia?"

Elijah paused briefly. "Two points. First, free trade agreements were somewhat useful—at least in making some rich people really *beep*-ing obscenely rich. But then Donald Trimp—" loud boos and hissing from audience "—decided not to trade within the rules of the agreements. The World Court at the Hague is powerless to force the USA to comply with these agreements, so let's pull our heads out of our collective asses and move on.

"Point two, all that free trade shit you said? I think it helps us realize that the governments in most countries use money—usually Gross Domestic Product or Gross National Product—as the almighty measuring stick. But GDP / GNP numbers are misleading—the majority of money measured in GDP stays in the big corporations, and with their shareholders. We should be measuring our success with a different measuring tool."

The minister looked sceptical. "Such as?"

"Gross National Happiness—GNH—is a better measurement tool." The audience applauded and whistled their approval. Elijah's guest looked less than impressed. Elijah plunged ahead cheerfully. "Let me explain. GNH measures not only the sum total of economic output, but also measures sustainability, the local and global environmental impact of a product or service being made, plus personal growth, education, personal freedoms and the mental and physical well being of citizens. Doesn't that sound better than just using money as the ultimate determining factor that measures our success?" Elijah smiled at his guest as the audience cheered and clapped.

The minister of trade shook her head. "What you are proposing isn't practical. Almost every country in the world uses GDP or GNP as a means of measuring economic success. I have read about GNH, but no major country on this planet serious about economic growth is using Gross National Happiness as a metric. It's not scientific, and it is very subjective."

Elijah put on his sad face. "If it makes you feel better," the minister continued, "the United Nations is studying GNH, and Canada has a member on a sixty-eight nation panel that is attempting to make this measurement more universally applicable. I'm not saying that GNH is a bad system, but right now, most of the countries in the world measure their economic output by GDP." Boos, catcalls and raspberries were the main response from the studio audience.

"Garsh, that does make me feel better," Elijah quipped in an aw-shucks voice. He sounded like the bastard child of Goofy and Sponge Bob. Then he smartly slapped himself across the face. "No, I'm kidding, " he spat out angrily. "I don't feel better at all. Because if money is the only *beep*-ing metric that determines our success, then we are going to really *beep* this planet up. "Elijah nodded offstage to his director, and a screen appeared over top of the host and his guest. Bullet points appeared on the screen as Elijah went on one of his famous rants. "Look, here is what we have achieved under NAFTA."

"Excessive pollution and environmental concerns—international corporations will put their factories in the countries with the lowest standards and regulation regarding pollution and the environment. Under NAFTA, numerous international companies relocated in Mexico from the USA and Canada, because Mexico had the least demanding environmental regulations. Under a new deal those companies will leave Mexico to relocate where? Somalia? Bangladesh? It's a race to the bottom!"

Elijah was standing now, flailing his arms, getting his groove on.

"Lowest wage workers—same as above. International corporations will put their factories in the countries with the lowest wage and worker benefits. Under NAFTA, numerous companies relocated in Mexico from the USA and Canada, because Mexico had the lowest wage workers. But surely, someone, somewhere must be willing to do more work for less money than Mexicans."

The minister of international trade was looking less and less happy as Elijah raved on.

"Unequal distribution of wealth. In 1984 the poorest 50 per cent of Canadians accounted for 5.7 per cent of our nation's assets or wealth—money, property, possessions. Today, the poorest 50 per cent of Canadians have 1.1 per cent of our national wealth. In 1984 the richest 10 per cent of our population owned 51 per cent of our national wealth. Today the richest 10 per cent of our population owns 68.5 per cent of the assets in Canada!"

The audience was really getting worked up now, standing, screaming, angry—visibly pissed off. "Wait, wait—it gets better," Elijah egged them on. "The richest 1 per cent of our citizens currently control 32 per cent of our nation's wealth." The minister was beginning to realize that Elijah's audience was made up from the lower 50 per cent of the economic pool, based on their reaction to this news.

"Okay, okay, calm down now." Elijah waved his arms to placate the crowd. "Our guest is not the enemy here. We are just having a discussion—an exchange of ideas if you will. I do have a guest who would like to speak to us about free trade. Canadian farmers tell us that more trade dollars does not equate to more individual prosperity. Let's hear from the Canadian Family Farms Union president, Charley Shackleton!"

The audience roared, whistled and whooped their approval as a picture of Charley in coveralls appeared on the studio screen. Charley was one of Elijah's most popular returning guests on the show. He was a big, lovable down-home sorta feller. He'd been on the show multiple times—well, Elijah and other guests would visit him on his small farm in Elgin County, Ontario. Or they'd send a TV crew to the farm to get an opinion piece. Charley wasn't the sort of feller who would be comfortable in a big-city studio.

The picture of Charley went live on a split screen, and the crowd noise increased.

"Charley, can you hear me?" Elijah asked.

"Sure can. The doctor told me just last week I got twenty-twenty hearing."

"Charley, I think your doctor meant…oh , never mind. Can you tell our viewers your thoughts on free trade?"

"Sure, but before we start is your beeping machine workin'? You know the one that beeps out bad words?"

"Yes, Charley, CBC makes sure of that—well, at least for my show they do." The audience hooted. "Why? Are you gonna be using bad words?"

"Oh heavens, no. There might be ladies and children watchin'. But you prob'ly will when you hear what I got to say."

"Okay, Charley. Now how about that free trade?"

"Well now, sir. For small farmers, free trade just means more money for fewer people. You see, since 1988, agricultural exports leaving Canada have tripled, but net farm income has fallen by 37 per cent."

The camera panned out to reveal that Charley had his notes written on a blackboard in his barn. In the background was a calf, a cow, and Charley's old dog, Fred, all peering intently at Charley and the blackboard like kids in a classroom.

"Now over that same period," Charley continued, "farm debt has doubled, 46 per cent of Canadian farmers have been forced off the land, the number of independent or family farmers has dropped by 68 per cent, and there are twenty-four thousand fewer jobs in the food processing industry. S'cuse me." Charley paused to loudly blow his nose into a handkerchief that was new in the 1970s. Elijah winced. "So this free trade agreement has increased trade volume, but it squeezed out a lot of the small to mid-size farms and farmers."

"So free trade is bad?" Elijah asked.

"Well, for most people, yes. Now, to be fair, it's been good to a few people I guess. Free trade helps Monsanto, Cargill, Pioneer, big oil and gas companies and large grocery store chains. But I don't personally know any of them folks."

"So, Charley, how do we fix this?" Elijah asked.

"Well, we need to look back at how things used to be." Fred barked. Pause.

"Extrapolate."

"Extrapa what?" The audience tittered

"Explain how things used to be, and why we might want to do things that way again."

"Well, why didn't you say so? Listen, here's how things used to be. They used to be small and simple. Used to be if you worked hard you could make an honest livin'. I took over this farm in 1967 from my daddy. It's a sixty-acre piece, by the way, and my family's been farming it since 1885."

The audience applauded. A picture of the original homestead appeared, followed by pictures of:

Charley's mother and father...

Charley as a baby. *Awwwww...*

And Charley's wedding. *Awwwww...*

Charley was live again on the split screen. "So way back BFT…"

"Sorry, Charley—what's BFT?" Elijah asked.

"Well, Before Free Trade, of course." Charley shook his head and smiled. "Try and keep up, son. So, BFT, 15 per cent of Canadians made their living from the three Fs—farmin', fishin' and forestry. We really didn't need big companies to act as middlemen, or to run an international market for us, or to bring in things from away. People bought the majority of their food from local farmers and small markets. So from this here farm, we grew some corn, or oats, or barley and had pasture land and hayfields. We used what we grew to feed our beef cattle, and then sold our beef to a local butcher. If we had more corn or hay than we needed for our animals sometimes we could sell that to neighboring farms. If not, it would keep. We also raised chickens, and sold the eggs, and if they didn't lay eggs, well, then we had a chicken dinner. We put in a big garden every year as well—what we didn't preserve for ourselves we would sell in town at the farmers' market—fresh beans, tomatoes, squash, punkins, potatoes, and so forth. S'cuse me. " Charley turned away to blow his nose again.

"Charley, what per cent of Canadians make their living from the three Fs today?

"Yeah, I was hopin' you'd ask that. It's 0.7 per cent." Charley looked sad. Fred barked. The cow and calf just kept eating hay and looking at Charley.

"Charley, what about other household things you needed to buy BFT? You know—clothes, soap, pots and pans, televisions, shoes, tools, cars, telephones, toothpaste, record players? Where did all that come from?

"Well, almost everything we needed was made local, or at least in our country. There was a factory just down the road here used to make good work boots. Free trade kicked the guts outta that, pardon my language, and sixty people lost their jobs. Every town had a butcher, a baker, a candlestick maker, tailors, blacksmiths, cobblers, coopers, carpenters, soap makers, weavers. There was local people who made clothes, or for fancier stuff you could order from Eaton's or Hudson's Bay. Most of what they sold was all the things you just described made by Canadians working in small factories. It might surprise your audience to learn that we used to make cars and televisions and telephones right here in this country. And what we made was good quality."

"So when did we start importing everything?

"Well, when free trade removed protective tariffs, that's when the arse really started to go out of 'er. And it's our fault—we let 'em, cause we wanted things cheaper. We voted with our wallets. So now all the things we used to make and the food we eat get made somewhere else—clothes, cars, household goods—well, just everything. Visit one of them horrible WilMart stores and tell me if you find anything local made. So those big corporations build factories wherever they can find the lowest wages and cheapest materials. Mix in big economies of scale and low fuel cost to keep it cheap and on the road."

"So how do we turn this around?"

"Seems pretty simple to me and Fred." Fred barked. "Get out of NAFTA, and don't sign TPP, or CETA, or any of 'em." Charley paused for a minute while Elijah tried to calm down the crowd, because they were cheering so loudly.

"If it ain't made here, or grown here, then we tax it. And make it hurt—like a 30 per cent or 50 per cent tax. Then use that tax revenue to give small start-up businesses low cost loans and tax breaks." Elijah paused for another break to let the crowd vent their emotions. "There's some pretty smart people out there—they'll figure out what needs to be made. Here's a hint—when everybody in your town is barefoot, might be a good time to set up a cobbler shop. When everybody starts to smell bad, maybe you could make some soap and sell it. No tomatoes in town? Well—" Charley scratched his nose "—you're smart kids. You'll figure it out."

"Charley, what you are suggesting sounds like what Mr Trimp—"boos, hisses, cat calls "—is proposing—eliminate free trade, put tariffs on imports and put local people back to work."

"Well, listen. On a personal level, I don't much like President Trimp. But even an arsehole like him can have one good idea. And him wiggling outta free trade deals will likely be some short-term pain for some long-term gain for our American neighbours."

"Thanks for this, Charley."

"Anytime. Say good night, Fred." Fred barked. Charley tipped his hat, and the live feed returned to the studio.

"So, Minister, do you see the average Canadians concern specifically regarding free trade?" Elijah continued. "We have been operating under NAFTA guidelines for twenty-two years. And things aren't getting better for the majority of Canadians, or for our trading partners. The gap between a very rich minority and a very poor majority of citizens continues to widen here, and in Mexico and the US of A. Look, can't you see? The timing is perfect for it—the Americans are not playing by the rules and want to end it as well. So let's beat them to the punch. What if we opted out of free trade and introduced tariffs on all imported goods?"

"Elijah, first—as much as we long for the good old days, there is no going back. Also, if you ask a lot of people in Charley's demographic, the "good old days" weren't all that good. Look, NAFTA is a binding international agreement, and the International Court of Justice would order Canada to pay trillions—not billions—trillions of dollars in punitive damages to opt out."

"Who would we owe that money to?"

"Well to the other NAFTA countries—the USA and Mexico, the World Bank…" the minister responded.

"And what if we just refused to pay it?" The audience went ballistic.

Cynthia Forlund was gobsmacked. Elijah was grinning like a madman. His audience was out of control—kind of like an Occupy rally, but better organized, with an agenda and a well-spoken popular leader. *Why did I agree to come here? These people are all certifiable whack jobs…*

"Elijah, what you are proposing is flat-out anarchy." The minister was interrupted by a ferocious roar of approval from the audience. *Try another tack—this group is okay with anarchy.* Elijah and the studio crew got the audience calm and reseated. With a gesture, he indicated that the floor was hers. The minister rose to speak, appealing to the audience.

"Canada is a highly respected nation. Our democratic system, our individual rights and freedoms, our standard of living is the envy of most other nations on the planet. We achieved this admirable level of international respect over a one-hundred-and-fifty-year tradition of honesty, trust and adherence to international law. Opting out of NAFTA is a ridiculous proposal, tantamount to committing national economic suicide." This was met with boos and curses. She waited them out. Most politicians learned early in the game that a thick skin was essential for survival.

"Then to suggest that we not only opt out of NAFTA, but also refuse to pay the penalties imposed by an international court, it's beyond absurd." More boos and curses.

"We would be cut off, isolated from the international community…" Yay, hoorah, she was interrupted by cheers of approval. The minister was visibly frustrated.

At a nod from his director, Elijah interceded. "Okay, okay, people. Like everyone in our current capitalistic construct, we need to pay some bills. Let's everybody chill, and enjoy this word from our sponsor.

The "advertisement" was a sixty-second satirical kick in the nuts. It began with a close up of a cheerful Elijah in a lab coat, hairnet and hardhat as the boss of a meat packing plant—Maple Loaf—introducing their latest product.

"Here at Maple Loaf Incorporated, we know what you want. Low prices. Introducing LoafaLot! LoafaLot is our new low fat, high protein affordable option to beef, pork and chicken. Our LoafaLot line of luncheon meat is made with choice cuts from slender foreign people who have no useful purpose. Don't worry, you don't know these people."

The camera panned out to show an assembly line of cheerful victims waving at the camera (portrayed by Elijah's regular cast of characters): elderly Africans, homeless children from the slums of Calcutta, malnourished kids from dumps in Rio. One by one, the assembly line dropped the people into a cartoonish grinder that turned them into pink slurry, and extruded them as luncheon meat with a happy face.

Lab-coated Elijah reappeared, smiling maniacally in a close up, assembly line still running in the background. "LoafaLot from Maple Loaf. Just try and find a lower priced lunch meat!"

The minister of trade was still grimacing from the satirical piece when an actual commercial from Maple Loaf Incorporated ran. She glanced at Elijah, who just smiled and winked. A make-up crew touched them both up.

"And we're back live in three, two, one…"

"Hey, welcome back. Our guest is Cynthia Forlund, Canada's minister of international trade. We have been discussing the pros and cons of free trade, and whether or not Canada should sign larger free trade agreements such as CETA and TPP."

The audience interrupted with chants and fist pumps: "No free trade! No free trade! No free trade! No free trade! No free trade!"

"All right, all right—be cool, bitches." Gradually, the chanting subsided, and the audience took their seats.

"Minister, we seem to agree to disagree on whether free trade is good or bad for us. So I have a proposal. This is a democracy—can we agree on that much?"

"Of course," the minister responded.

"Good. So as I recall, a democracy is defined as a form of government in which the power is vested in the people, and exercised by the people directly or indirectly through elected representatives. Still with me?"

"Yes, of course, but what has that got to do—"

"Well, that's the lead-up for my proposal," Elijah interrupted. "If democracy literally means 'power to the people' let's practise it in its purest form. Hold a referendum, and let the people decide—"

Now the crowd interrupted Elijah with the biggest cheer yet.

"As I was saying, let the people decide. Free trade—yes or no? If you let us—the people—decide, and we make a bad decision—you're off the hook! We can't even blame you if it all goes horribly wrong. Great idea, no?"

"No." The minister stood up angrily. "Your proposal is ridiculous. There is no democracy in the world today that makes decisions this way. The reason that we have elected representatives is to allow these representatives time. Time to perform a detailed study of laws and proposals, time to apply evidence based decision-making processes, and time to rationally debate the issues within a parliamentary framework prior to voting."

She moved to the front of the stage, appealing to the crowd. "The average Canadian has neither the time nor the inclination to read the regulatory framework of a trade agreement. For heaven's sakes, the TPP draft in English is eleven thousand pages without annexes and appendices. The French draft is 50 per cent bigger! Do any of you really want to slog through that?" The minister was clearly getting frustrated.

Elijah hugged her and patted her back. "There, there, it'll be okay. We know that you are under a lot of pressure. It's not your fault—you are trapped in a broken system. Let us help you carry that burden, sister."

He turned to the audience. "The minister has made one good point, though. I tried to read the TPP draft it's a sure-fire cure for insomnia." Laughs and groans from audience.

"But here's the thing—we don't need to read the proposed deal to know it's not good for us. Our life experience through the past twenty years tells us that NAFTA has made corporations and shareholders rich, and poor people poorer." Screams of approval from the studio audience.

"And life has kicked us in the nuts and in the lady balls so many times, we know it's a bad deal without reading eleven thousand pages of legalese and gobbledegook." Bigger cheers.

"Listen, Cynthia—you've been a good sport here today. We just hope that you will consider some of what we have told you here. We hope that you can find the courage to suggest a referendum on free trade to our prime minister." The minister of trade did not look like a woman convinced. Elijah turned for the big finish close-up. "Hey, remember as a kid, when you really wanted something, you would ask Mom? And then if Mom said no, you'd ask Dad?

"Do it. Ask Daddy."

"Yesssssssss," the audience responded.

"Dustin, Mr. Prime Minister, Dad—I know you watch our show. Let us help you. Empower us. You are scaring us with all this free trade talk about CETA. We are afraid that you, our elected representatives, are going to sign new free trade agreements. But we don't want that. When I say we, I mean we the people who don't own corporations, or contribute to a political party. We are offering you a tremendous opportunity. Let us vote on free trade. Give us a referendum on that topic. Instead of your government taking the blame for stupid decisions, let us make some stupid decisions with you. We might even make the right decision. Can you imagine the group hug if that happened?

"Thanks for listening, Canada. My name is Elijah, and it's my privilege to be your host on…"

Elijah held a microphone out to the audience, who responded rather vigorously: "Power to the People! Power to the People! Power to the People! Power to the People!."

"And cut…bring up the house lights"

The audience filed out, still buzzing like a beehive that just got whacked with a stick. Quite a few of them stayed behind, hoping to get a photo with Elijah or an invite backstage, or to try and make out with him… Elijah did have rock star status after all, and his following was very young, often high, and not very shy. The supporting cast, tech support and stage crew didn't mind. Sometimes they could even scoop up the leftovers.

Elijah was already back in his office, arguing with CBC management. "We just had a call from Maple Loaf Foods," the VP of advertising was saying. "They are threatening to pull out as our major sponsor." Another corporate suit from head office was weighing in as well. "The LoafaLot skit was disgusting. We are getting hundreds of complaints from viewers."

"Hey, I've got a good idea," interrupted Elijah angrily. "Why don't you ass-clowns terminate my contract if you're so unhappy, and then you can have some thoughtful polite boring guy like Peter Bridgeman take over the hottest talk show in recent memory." The suits looked surprised.

This certainly was not normal CBC behavior. "Because our ratings are through the roof, that's why you won't do it," continued Elijah, as he held the door open for the execs. "Thank you very much, gentlemen. It's always a pleasure speaking with you."

CHAPTER 5.
The Uncomfortable Pension Plan Dilemma

Most people think of universities as institutes of higher learning.

Sure, some of them focus on that. But first and foremost, universities are factories that produce graduates. The students pay the university to teach them until they receive a degree. Those universities who can charge their customers the most money, and control their costs—staff, building maintenance, heat, lights, etc.—can realize a profit and remain in business. On the flip side, the customers (students) were willing to pay for a degree because people with university degrees were traditionally better paid than those persons without post-secondary education. At least, that was pretty much how it had worked for the past sixty years or so. Until recently.

Unfortunately, the economic situation all around the world had been pretty far from normal since mid-2017. This was causing significant concern in almost every business in the world, including universities. Enrolment was declining dramatically in all Western countries. Consider the situation St. Mary's was in. Typically, St. Mary's enrolled 7500 students each year, with 4000 of those students coming from countries outside Canada. Every Canadian university tried their best to attract foreign students because foreign students paid the most tuition. (They also tended to live in the university's residences and take out meal plans which added revenue to the school's bottom line.) Students from Canada paid less tuition than foreign students, and the government subsidized the difference in cost for those Canadian students. This subsidy was expensive, but an investment in education was normally viewed as a smart thing to do.

The recent economic downturn had priced a university education out of reach for some young people, regardless of nationality. Both the provincial and federal governments were considering reducing the subsidies that they provided to universities. Parents who might have paid for their children's education a few years ago had seen their pension funds and investments significantly reduced when the stock markets crashed in 2017.

Classes at St. Mary's and most other universities were finished their spring semester. Benjamin Big Canoe had heard rumours that he might be kept on staff, but he had built up two weeks' vacation in any case. It was his last day of work, but he had already finished everything he needed to do. He did need to see his mentor, though.

"Dr. MacAllister?"

"Yes, Ben. Come in. Que pasa?"

"I picked up our mail." Ben handed Professor MacAllister his letter. "There was one letter for each of us, both from the same address—our pension fund managers. Mine isn't good news, but I'm curious to see if your letter says the same thing."

"Well, let's have a look." MacAllister opened his letter with a letter opener his father gave him when he completed his PhD thirty years ago. It was a miniature sword with the Clan MacAllister insignia on it.

Alex MacAllister adjusted his glasses and began to read aloud.

"Dear: Professor MacAllister:

Please be advised that the recent global economic downturn has negatively affected the pension fund of St. Mary's University employees. In order to conserve funds in the plan over the long term, the following changes will be implemented immediately:

Pension payouts will be reduced by 15%, and contributions to the plan will increase by 7.5 %.

We regret that these changes are necessary…

These percentages may be adjusted as the market fluctuates…

We trust that these changes are only temporary…"

The letter droned on with some more corporate legalese.

"This is bullshit!," MacAllister shouted. He was quickly turning an alarming shade of crimson.

"Are you okay?" Benjamin asked his mentor. He hadn't seen the elderly professor display much in the way of emotion in the few months they'd worked together. *I hope I remember my CPR, 'cause this guy looks like he might need it.*

"No- I'm pretty far from okay." MacAllister reached into his bottom drawer and bought out a bottle of Scotch and two glasses.

"Not for me, thanks," Ben said, checking his watch. It was nine a.m.

"Suit yourself," grunted MacAllister. He poured two generous fingers in each glass, and added a tiny bit of water. "You're guilty by association, anyway, if anyone else comes in the office."

"That's a good point," Ben said. He reached across the desk and winked at MacAllister as he took a sip of Scotch. He made an awful grimace as the whisky burned its way down his throat. "So, tell me, why does that letter upset you so much? I mean, it's only money."

MacAllister sighed. "Yeah, I used to think like that in the 1970s, Ben. I've been paying into that pension plan for almost thirty years. By last year's estimates I was going to receive sixty thousand dollars a year." He shook the letter angrily. "And now these assholes tell me that I'm only going to get fifty-one thousand? Unacceptable." He paused for a sip of whisky.

Ben was going to speak, but the older professor wasn't finished. "Look, I was married twice. Being divorced is expensive. Doing it twice, well, let's just say I don't have a lot of savings to fall back on. So a 15 per cent reduction in my pension is the shittiest news I've had in a long time. I can't afford the mortgage on the house I'm living in now, and I can't sell it. My settlement with my second wife is still in proceedings, but that's not going well, either." MacAllister fell silent.

The two men sat quietly for a minute. "Yeah, it sucks from my perspective, as well." Benjamin admitted as he studied his copy of the letter. He punched some numbers into the calculator on his phone. "So, I'm already paying 8 per cent of my salary into this pension plan. This increase takes that up to 15.5 per cent. The office was quiet again for a minute, as each man took a small sip of Scotch, lost in his thoughts.

"Alex, I can't afford to pay into this pension plan. I'm afraid it won't exist in a few years."

Dr. MacAllister nodded sadly. "I understand your concern, but, if you want to teach here, you have to be a union member, and you have to contribute to the pension plan. It's not voluntary."

"Alex, I do like teaching here. And this letter isn't the only reason I'm saying this, but, I'm going to submit my resignation."

If possible, Alex MacAllister looked sadder than before, but then he seemed to pull himself together. "Maybe before you resign, you should hear this offer. The dean wants you to join our department as a full professor with tenure. He and I just discussed this yesterday. You'd be our youngest prof. And I predict you would be head of this department within a few years. It's a good career, Benjamin. I mean, this is what you've been working toward, yes?"

Benjamin smiled softly, shaking his head. "Alex, I'm honoured to be offered a position as a professor. And yes, it is what I have been working toward. A few years ago, I would have jumped all over this opportunity."

"But now?"

"But now I have to turn down the offer." Dr. MacAllister was going to interject, but Benjamin spoke first. "Alex, it's not about this pension money. And your offer of tenure is so cool—I wish I could take it. But I've been talking with some old friends, and we are going to try something a little different."

"May I ask what you are going to do?"

Benjamin stood and tossed back the remainder of the whisky in his glass. "I can't be too specific, because it might not even get off the ground. Let's just say we are gonna try and shake shit up a little."

Professor MacAllister stood as well, and grimly offered Benjamin his hand, but the younger man walked around the desk and gave the older professor a big hug. "Hey, I'm around for a couple weeks yet. I'll see you again before I go."

Benjamin was almost at the door when he turned again. "Oh, and Dr. MacAllister?"

"Yes, Dr. Big Canoe?"

"Thanks for everything. I learned a lot from you."

"Benjamin, you have it backwards." Ben looked quizzically at MacAllister. "It was I who learned from you." Benjamin was about to speak, but the older professor put up his hand in a stop sign. "Now get outta here before I start crying."

Benjamin closed the door softly behind him, and his cellphone rang.

"Hey, Elijah. How are you doing brother?"

"I'm all good, man. Great to hear your voice again. Listen, as I hoped, we're done shooting till two p.m. tomorrow. So today's meeting is all lined up."

"I'm all in. Where are you? Do you need a lift?"

"Sure. I'm at the CBC studio on Summer Street. You know it?"

"I'm there in five minutes."

Moments later, Benjamin Big Canoe and his former roommate Elijah exchanged their ritual "Loyal Order of the Water Buffalo" secret handshake. It was like the worst uncoordinated version of cool secret handshakes ever. (Note: To see the original version, you need to watch The *Flintstones*. Not right now, though, keep reading.)

"C'mon, I booked us a work room in a private spot—we can work there, and the food is great. You know the Henry House?"

The Henry House had a third-floor private room that suited their needs perfectly. There were already fifteen or more people in the room when Benjamin and Elijah arrived.

"Hey, let's all grab a seat and we'll get this started," Elijah suggested. Benjamin took a seat beside Juliette Sparks.

"Do you know how you got here, Grasshopper?" he asked his former student quietly.

"Well, sir, I got this email invite from Elijah, and he said he read a paper I wrote, but I never met the dude, so… uh, no, I don't know how I got here, but this is cool."

Benjamin grinned. "Yeah, that was a good paper on political reform. I sent it to Elijah, and he told me he was gonna invite you to this meeting."

"Okay, it occurs to me we don't all know each other," Elijah began. "So, I'm Elijah. I work in television." The assembly giggled. They knew who he was. Elijah pointed at his old friend. "Go, Ben."

"Benjamin Big Canoe. I'm a teacher and a student."

"Juliette Sparks. President, St. Mary's University Student Council."

"Siobahn O'Meara. I used to catch fish, till greedy short-sighted assholes took them all."

"Less Izmore. I was a banker long ago, but I live in a commune now."

"Annette Arsenault, Farmer."

"Danni Grey Eyes. I'm Chief of Mistawasis First Nation in Saskatchewan."

"Andre Silverberg. I was a doctor, then I was a prisoner. I may be a doctor again soon. Thanks to those of you who may have shortened my stay in prison." He looked pointedly at Elijah, who winked back. Dr. Silverberg's story was well known. He had done four years in prison for helping people with medically assisted death.

As introductions continued, waiters brought in a variety of food: some kick-ass seafood platters, a variety of vegetable trays, cheese boards, charcuterie plates and sandwiches. Two more waiters arrived with tasting boards of the pub's house-made beers and ales. There was wine on the table, and pitchers of water.

Elijah kept the meeting going. "Okay, good to meet everybody. Listen. I'm starving. Dig in, we got all afternoon. You need something vegan? Dairy-free? Whatever—ask our hosts here, they'll hook you up. It's on me. Don't sweat the money part."

After some minutes of serious dining, Elijah addressed the group again. "Okay, listen, keep eating and drinking. It's a working lunch after all. Our new friend Juliette chose this venue for our meeting because it's full of history. And I hope you love history as much as Juliette and I seem to. Tell us a bit about Henry House, mademoiselle."

Juliette stood up confidently. She was a strikingly beautiful girl, with mocha skin and a tremendous seventies'-style Afro. She was also a very poised speaker.

"William Alexander Henry was a former owner of this house. Mr. Henry was, among other things: a Father of Canadian Confederation, a co-author of the British North America Act, an attorney general, a member of the Nova Scotia House of Assembly; a mayor of Halifax, and a justice of the Supreme Court of Canada."

Juliette paused to take a sip of beer. And looked around the room at each person as she continued speaking.

"I'm very proud to be from Halifax, and I'm glad that Elijah asked me to choose a venue for this meeting. Think about what tremendous things the former owner of this house accomplished. The British North America Act? A Father of Confederation? John A. MacDonald always stayed here when he was in Halifax. Can you imagine what Sir John A. and William Henry and their like-minded friends discussed over multiple glasses of whisky?"

Juliette paused and walked around the table as she continued speaking.

"I like to imagine that they discussed how to build a free and prosperous nation. And they did a tremendous job. You just have to travel elsewhere to realize how blessed we are to be Canadians. The reason we are meeting here today is to discuss ways that we can make Canada a much, much better place to live. Our political system just needs a few tweaks to make it better. And what better place to discuss how that might be achieved than in a room in which many of the original plans for our country were drawn out."

Juliette raised her glass. "So welcome to Henry House. Welcome to Halifax. And join me please in a toast." Chairs scraped as the group stood.

"To a new and improved Canada."

"To a new and improved Canada." The group responded, clinking glasses.

The meeting lasted about eight hours. It was brainstorming at its finest. They went machine-gun fire around the table, and every idea was written down on a whiteboard. There was no criticism of any idea: nothing was to be considered crazy or impossible. "Dream big, bitches," Elijah encouraged as he chaired the meeting.

After an hour, the group was exhausted of ideas. They took a health break, then discussed the ideas in detail—dissecting them, critiquing them, tweaking them. It was an eclectic group.

Each person was extremely passionate and energetic. But after seven hours of discussion the groups energy level was getting lower.

Elijah called the meeting at 8:30 p.m., and promised to stay in touch regarding further action. Folks began to drift away in ones and twos

Benjamin and Elijah had a good buzz going. Danni didn't drink, but she could spend time in the company of drinkers without feeling awkward. Juliette had consumed an astonishing amount of beer but somehow still walked and spoke in complete sentences. They were the last four in the room.

"Folks, it's only nine o'clock," Juliette informed them. "Now what?"

"Are there any party spots in Halifax?" Elijah asked with a wry smile.

"Excuse me?" Juliette responded. "Just try and keep up okay?"

Going anywhere publicly with Elijah was always crazy. He was mobbed everywhere they went. By eleven p.m. there were girls drinking tequila belly-button shots from his navel, and boys doing the same from Juliette's. Benjamin learned long ago not to try and keep up with Elijah. He had been drinking water most of the night since leaving Henry House.

A shirtless Elijah and almost shirtless Juliette were leading a conga line dance around the seventh (or eighth?) bar when Danni suggested to Benjamin that they should consider calling it a night.

In response, Benjamin gently grabbed her hand and escorted her back on to a throbbing dance floor. Elijah shimmied his way over to them.

"My brother, I am fading fast," he said in Benjamin's ear. "Do we have an exit strategy from this madhouse?"

"Yeah, Danni and I were just discussing that very issue. I have lots of room at my place for all of us."

"Can we bring that beautiful girl, as well?" Elijah asked, motioning to Juliette, who was dancing with a crowd of admirers.

Benjamin looked at Elijah and smiled." Of course. Danni, try and get Elijah to the door. I'll get Juliette."

Benjamin rescued Juliette from a crowd of admirers, and put his coat over her shoulders as they stepped outside. Danni gave her sweater to Elijah, who had been shirtless since the belly-shot bar.

"It's only five minutes to my place," Benjamin informed the gang. "Do we wanna cab it? Or can you walk?"

"I'm good to walk," Elijah stated defiantly. "Lead on, Brother Benjamin. I just needed some fresh air." He fired up a blunt and put his arm around Juliette.

Benjamin was a wonderfully gracious host. Once he had Elijah and Juliette safely tucked in bed, he returned to Danni in the living room. She was watching *South Park*. He rolled a joint, lit it, took a hit and passed it to Danni. She was the most beautiful person he had ever seen.

They smoked quietly for a few minutes while giggling at *South Park*'s "Blame Canada" episode.

Danni's hair was so black there was a sheen of purple to it. "Danni, do you have a boyf—"

Danni cut him off. It was quiet for a couple minutes.

"If I had a boyfriend, would I kiss you like that?"

CHAPTER 6.
Shaking Shit Up

"Welcome to *NBC Nightly News* from our New York Headquarters. Our lead story tonight is taking place in Canada, where a new political party is shaking the very foundations of traditional Canadian politics. The Independent People's Party, headed by a popular talk show host..."

Click

"...This new party is being enthusiastically embraced by Gen X, Gen Y and the millennials, and has captured the attention of baby boomers in the lower-earning brackets," a British broadcaster was saying to his guest, an expert on constitutional monarchies. "Can you explain to our viewers why the wealthier and financially established people in Canada seem frightened by this new party's platform?"

Click

"...Our next story follows the meteoric rise of the Independent People's Party in Canada," Peter Bridgeman was saying to Canadian Broadcasting Corporation viewers. "Our guest tonight is no stranger to television—he is the host of the most popular television show in Canadian history. Elijah, welcome," Peter said, shaking the younger man's hand as they both took a seat facing each other.

"Thanks for having me on *The National*, Peter."

"Tell us, why did you start the Independent People's Party?"

"Well, Peter, first, let me say that I didn't start it—a lot of really smart people from many varied backgrounds suggested it and asked me to lead it. But those people wanted to start the party because we believe that our current political system is badly broken. For one hundred and fifty years Canadians have had federal governments lead by either the Conservative or Liberal Party. This system of political parties does not allow for the best ideas to flourish.

"Let's assume for a minute that you are a Liberal MP and I am a Conservative MP. Our parties dictate that the other parties' ideas and platforms are always wrong and bad. So, essentially we will spend four years shouting at each other in a dysfunctional Parliament. If you have a good idea, I can't support it, because we are from different parties.

"Over the past one hundred and fifty years as a nation, we elected Conservatives to fix a Liberal mess, and then elected Liberals to fix a Conservative mess, and then elected—well, I think our viewers get the picture. But no one can fix anything very well, because the system is f—flawed." Elijah paused and smiled as Peter Bridgeman flinched, clearly worried that his guest would use the F-word on CBC news.

"Some people are comparing you and the Independent Party to Donald Trimp—you are both newcomers to politics, both of you are well known via television and social media, both of you are promising radical change. How do you react to that?"

"Ouch." Elijah winced and hugged himself. "Yeah, that one hurts, Peter. Because Donald Trimp is currently the most uninformed, out of touch, dangerous racist alive today. In the simplest terms, here is how we differ. Donald Trimp is a huge *beep*-hole and I, Elijah, am not. Now, notwithstanding what a complete and total *beep*-head Mr. Trimp is, The Donald and I do share two common beliefs." Elijah held up a finger.

"One, Western political systems are currently broken. And, two, these systems can only be repaired by a new person or party willing to enact significant—dare I say radical—change that brings about positive change for common people."

The host looked thoughtfully perplexed with a finger to his upper lip. It was his trademark look when wishing to appear thoughtfully perplexed. "But that attempt at radical change hasn't worked well in America." Bridgeman pointed out to his guest. "Since November 2016 there have been record high instances of civil unrest, the American economy is in a recession or depression, the rate of unemployment has doubled, the—"

"Peter, I think we can all agree that Trimp's attempt at fixing a broken political system has been disastrous. Now remember, here is how we are fundamentally different." Elijah held his hands wide apart.

"Trimp—a *beep*-HOLE. Elijah—not a *beep*-HOLE."

In spite of himself, Bridgeman smiled wryly.

Elijah continued. "Peter, Mr. Trimp had no plan to fix a broken system. He appealed to downtrodden people that wanted change. He's a huckster, a con man, a fraud, a shyster. He's the bastard child of P.T Barnum and Mr. Haney from Green Acres. On a side note, it is frightening to most of the world that 47 per cent of the American people who voted in 2016 wanted change badly enough to vote for such an arrogant, uninformed, entitled bully." He fell to his knees, arms raised and appealed to the heavens. "What were you people thinking?"

Elijah returned to his chair opposite Peter Bridgeman. "Sadly, once elected, all that happened were Democrat crooks and lobbyists were replaced with Republican crooks and lobbyists. Two years from now, the people in America will likely elect the Democrats, in hopes that they can fix a Republican mess." Elijah shook his head and shrugged. "That isn't change. Same whore, different dress."

"So how does the Independent People's Party propose to fix what you are saying is a 'broken' political system?"

"A good question, Peter. So if the IPP is elected to form government, the first thing we intend to do is change the system so that political parties are dissolved or, at best, rendered impotent." The host was clearly ready to interject at this point, but Elijah held him off with an open hand, laughing.

"Trust me, Peter, we see the irony in this situation. In our current electoral system, the leader of the party who wins the most seats forms government. So, we have to first form a political party to win governance to then weaken political parties so that independent persons can represent

Canadians without having to blindly follow party direction. The only other way to effect any meaningful change in our political system would be a violent and bloody revolution." Elijah paused while the cameras shifted.

"But that seems so un-Canadian, and I'm the wrong guy to lead that charge. I'm a lover, not a fighter. So we thought we'd try the peaceful, less violent, approach first." Elijah paused briefly. "Oh yeah, there is another important change we are proposing to improve our current system of governance. We will also propose that an elected political position may not be held by the same person for more than four years."

"Why? What possible benefit do you see in placing a time limit on elected officials?" Peter Bridgeman now looked confused. It wasn't one of his trademark looks—he now seemed genuinely confused.

"It's simple, Peter. Politicians in our current system want two things, and two things only." Elijah held up two fingers to highlight his points. "Number one, to get personally re-elected, and number two, to keep their party in power.

"Peter, this consumes all their energy. By limiting time in political office to four years, and by eliminating the group-think of political parties as we propose, we have a system in which people run for office because they genuinely want to build a better country—not because they want a lifelong political career.

"Professional politicians who serve for multiple terms accumulate too much power over time and, eventually, that power will corrupt them in one way or another. They'll use that power to benefit a friend with a big government contract, who then hires their nephew, or gives kickbacks to the politician one way or another—perhaps by suggesting that the people who work for him should vote for the politician who got them the juicy contract. Also, in our current system, politicians are handsomely compensated with a good salary, a gold plated—but unsustainable—pension plan, and some rather remarkable perks."

"You mentioned the pension plan for members of Parliament a moment ago. What does your party—" Bridgeman paused to smile ironically "—that won't be a party if you get elected to government—propose to do with the pension plan for MPs?"

"I'd like to see it significantly reduced and the money in the pension plan put toward a minimum living allowance for all Canadians. But I wouldn't force other members of the IPP to follow that line—maybe they'd have some better ideas. I'm pretty sure if we asked Canadians of voting age what to do with it, and put it to a referendum, it wouldn't stay like it is."

"What other changes would the Independent People's Party propose?' the host asked.

"Well, remember, Peter—these are *proposals*, not *promises*." Elijah took great care to emphasize the difference between the two. "Because once we are elected, these Independent MPs will be acting in the best interest of their constituents, versus what I or a party whip tells them. So the short list of proposed changes?" Elijah leaned forward as the camera zoomed in.

"Tax carbon users. Heavily.

"Punish polluters harshly—through their wallets—and reward renewable energy users and innovators with tax breaks.

"Get Canada out of NAFTA and TPP trade agreements. Then heavily tax goods not made in Canada, and use that tax revenue to put Canadians back to work making all the things we now import.

"Give land grants to anyone who wants to start a farm, and subsidize them if necessary with a tax on imported food.

"Place a massive luxury tax on junk food, processed food, pop, etcetera, and use that revenue to further enhance health care and production of locally grown healthy foods.

"Legalize and sell good quality pot grown to a government standard and tax it like liquor.

"Reform the Senate to include election of independent senators, again, only up to four years in office.

"Is that enough for starters, or…?" Elijah leaned back in his chair, grinning.

"That is a lot of change. Surely you are aware that your proposals are being branded as radical, illegal and dangerous," Bridgeman mused wryly. "Do you believe Canadians are ready to embrace change on this level?"

Elijah smiled into the camera. "Well, Peter, the only people afraid of our proposals for change and labelling them as illegal or dangerous are the political bourgeoisies and the very wealthy—the well-established and the well-connected in society. Most people who fit that description are baby boomers. Currently, that demographic group has all the money, all the jobs, all the corporations, all the property, all the power."

Bridgeman was an accomplished journalist and host. He knew when to let his guests get on a roll. The cameras shifted again as Elijah continued his pitch.

"Peter, baby boomers have 90 per cent of the wealth in this and many other Western countries. Look, essentially Canadians have two choices in this election. We can either embrace change, and lead change by voting for independent-minded politicians, or do what we have always done for the last one hundred and fifty years, and elect a Conservative or Liberal government and hope for different results."

"Doing the same thing over and over and expecting different results. Is that Einstein?" the host asked his guest.

"Yes, sir. It's a cliché used to define insanity, attributed to Einstein. Personally, I think it's a better definition of stupidity than insanity, but, hey, neither trait is desirable."

The camera switched to a close-up of Peter Bridgeman, as he leaned forward in his chair. "Elijah, this has been very interesting. Last question. Do you really believe that the Independent People's Party has any chance of getting any members elected or forming government?"

"Well, Peter, the election is in nine months. And you normally lead the team that reports on elections as the ballots are counted, so, I look forward to hearing from you about our upset victory on election night. Thanks for having me." The lights dimmed and cameras faded out as the two shook hands.

The interview between Peter Bridgeman and Elijah was breaking the Internet. Similar interviews were happening all across Canada with people running for elected office in the next federal election as Independent members. The

Independent candidates were…different. Most were under thirty-five. They were farmers and fishermen, hippies and soldiers, lumberjacks and teachers. Very few were lawyers.

The day after the interview, Prime Minister Dustin Trudel was being briefed by his communications team on election issues. In the first twenty-five minutes they discussed their opposing political party's strategies and platforms. Included near the end of the brief was the Elijah interview, followed by snippets of interviews or press releases by various Independent candidates.

"In an interview today with Benjamin Big Canoe, a former associate professor of political science, and an Independent candidate for the riding of Nipissing-Timiskaming…"

"Independent hopeful Juliette Sparks, the twenty-two-year-old president of her student union at St Mary's University, announced her candidacy today in Halifax for the upcoming federal election. If elected, Ms Sparks would be one of the youngest…"

"Less Izmore, an elder from a commune called SimpleTown in British Columbia, is scoring some major points against the traditional political parties while running for the Independent People's Party…"

"In Quebec City, a former inmate of a federal prison announced his intentions to run as an Independent candidate in the upcoming federal election. Dr. Andre Silverberg, who served four years in prison for…"

Click. The screen froze.

John Isenor, the communications team lead, stood up to speak.

"Sir, this is a sampling of what Elijah and this band of…uhh, misfits are up to. Other than a popular talk show host, the remainder of the candidates are unknowns, neophytes and ne'er-do-wells. We don't believe that they pose a serious threat to our re-election, but—"

"John, I disagree." The prime minister interrupted curtly, standing up. "I believe that this group poses a very real threat to our party. They are offering people change during a time when the public perception is that everything in our society is broken. Look at what happened in 2016 in the USA. A political neophyte and absolute asshole promised Americans change, and he won the election." Trudel was standing, rocking gently from left to right.

"These IPP members have a unique platform, and a grassroots movement, especially among younger voters. We can't underestimate these people, or the message they are bringing. I want the IPP included in all our team briefs in the run-up to the election. Most importantly, I want a short bio on each of their candidates presented to this group one week from now."

One of the prime minister's executive assistants leaned in to speak quietly with the PM, who nodded affirmatively. "Till next week, John."

The prime minister had time to rise and stretch as his communications team left the briefing room and the finance minister filed in with his team, who all looked rather grim. *There is no good news coming in this brief,* the prime minister thought to himself as he took his seat. "What have you got, Robert?" he asked in what he hoped was a voice that conveyed optimism.

Unfortunately, the finance minister's brief contained very few reasons to be optimistic. The brief encapsulated a myriad of financial difficulties the country was facing. Robert Mornay began his brief with a very unpleasant fact.

"Sir, nationally, unemployment has risen to 17 per cent—the highest level since the Great Depression."

I wonder why they called it "Great"? the PM pondered, his mind wandering. *It didn't sound great in the history books....focus on the brief.* Dustin Trudel shook his head and forced himself back to the current reality of Bob Mornay's briefing.

"...As interest rates continue to rise, we are facing crippling costs in servicing our debt..."

"...Percentage of Canadians declaring personal bankruptcy is up 4 per cent over the previous year, and percentage of Canadian businesses declaring bankruptcy up 6 per cent..."

"...The committee recommends we lower Canadian Pension Plan payouts by..."

I wonder what a migraine feels like? Prime Minister Trudel had never had a migraine headache before, but he didn't feel very well. As the finance minister droned on about bad news without end on all matters financial, the PM feigned interest, simultaneously wishing to dim the lights and fighting the urge to vomit.

Mercifully, Robert Mornay was wrapping up his brief. "Sir, do you have any questions?"

"N...no, Bob, thank you, that'll be all. If you forward the brief to me I'll review it again as soon as I can."

As the finance minister and staff were leaving, the prime minister's aide leaned in again. "Sir, the minister of defence is next. You have about five minutes for a stretch and health break."

"Sorry, Jim. Please reschedule that brief." The prime minister checked his watch again. *Just enough time if I hurry.* "I have some other personal matters that just came up. Please call up my car."

Once in the black sedan, Dustin Trudel called his wife. "Hey, it's your husband…Well, I wasn't sure that you would recognize my voice…. Yeah, I'll pick them up…. Uh, huh…. We'll see you in about twenty minutes."

The prime minister was quite a hit at the kids' school. They usually got picked up by one of the family staff and/or Mrs. Trudel plus security personnel. His youngest daughter, Eugenie, sat in the front seat in her child seat and coerced the plainclothes RCMP driver into playing "I Spy" while they returned to the prime minister's residence. After supper, they played a board game at the kitchen table.

Shortly after eight o'clock, Sophia Trudel went upstairs to check on bedtime routines. Her two eldest, Xanadu and Estelle, were doing homework, or something to that effect on their laptops. "Lights out at nine o'clock, yes?" Sophia reminded the pair. She got a nod from her son, and an eye-roll from her daughter.

In Eugenie's room, she could hear her youngest talking to someone. She opened the door slowly to see Eugenie reading a children's story to her father. Prime Minister Dustin Trudel was sound asleep.

CHAPTER 7.
A Visit to SimpleTown

Donald Trimp was not enjoying his new job very much anymore.

Sure, it was fun for the first few weeks after his election, but that honeymoon period seemed like a long time ago. Trimp was already being vilified by the liberal media when he announced his candidacy, then even more so when he won the Republican nomination. During the race to the White House, it seemed like he got more bad press than anyone ever in the history of history. But all of that paled in comparison to the pounding he took since becoming POTUS. Little old church ladies now wrote him letters encouraging him to take his own life. Americans who were unable to travel outside their borders for fear of being attacked prayed publicly for his death.

Of course, The Donald only needed to look in a ridiculously oversized and extremely tacky gold-plated mirror to see who was responsible for this all of this. He had always been impetuous and extremely arrogant: he spoke without thinking, and often opined on policies he knew nothing about. Consider this.

He knew more about ISIS than all his army's generals and their intelligence teams.

He knew more about climate change than hundreds of climate scientists.

He knew more about national security threats than the FBI and CIA.

His remarks toward Latinos, Blacks, Muslims and immigrants easily won him the heavyweight title for "Racist of the Century."

His history of pussy-grabbing, his position on women's rights and his position regarding pregnancy as an inconvenience to employers saw him rightfully labelled as a chauvinist pig.

His denial of climate change and willingness to rape the planet for American jobs and profit for his friends (the 1 per cent) made him the largest threat the planet had ever known from an environmental perspective.

His disastrous management of free trade discussions had imploded the US and global economy. The fact that he had access to nuclear weapons codes, and was easily offended made a lot of people nervous, so the Russians and Chinese were assembling nuclear weapons at a tremendous pace.

There was a bigger list of stupid impulsive things The Donald had done in the past eighteen months, but you get the picture. According to his most outspoken detractors, "Orange Hitler" (one of his many nicknames) was soon going to replace the real Führer as the most hated and vilified person ever.

"Donald Trimp hasn't killed anyone," the Trimpanzees argued. "How dare you compare him to Hitler." Trimp's detractors argued that The Donald just needed a bit more time and a flock of blind, unquestioning followers in order to achieve Hitlerian heights.

In short: it really, really sucked to be Donald Trimp.

But his position was not unique: the political leaders in almost every country on the planet (even the ones who weren't racist, sexist, arrogant, uninformed, narcissist assholes) were reeling from an endless series of economic blows. Of course, the countries that had the strongest economies and the highest standards of living were feeling the pain the most. The economy of every G20 nation was in the toilet. Not surprisingly, those countries who traditionally had poor economies and the lowest standards of living on the planet as measured by traditional GDP methods were blissfully unaware of the recent global economic downturn.

In 2014, the poorest countries in the world as ranked by Gross Domestic Productivity were: Malawi, Burundi, the Central African Republic, Niger, Liberia, Madagascar, the Congo, Gambia, Ethiopia and Guinea. For the residents of these countries and some of the poorer nations on earth—the bottom eighty of one hundred and eighty ranked countries—not much had changed. They hadn't lost their job as companies declared bankruptcy, or seen their mortgage payment rise 33 per cent while the value of their home plummeted by the same percentage amount. Nor had their pensions been reduced or eliminated, or their electrical and fuel costs risen dramatically. The people who had lived the simplest lives had not fallen far, and thus, were not badly bruised. (It still sucked to live in those countries, but at least their citizens weren't whining about it. They had never known a life that didn't suck.)

The suicide rates in the poor countries certainly wasn't rising at an alarming rate: at least in comparison to the G20 nations. Of course, the poorer countries in the world had never established such a thing as a study on suicide rates at any time. Who could afford such luxury?

People in Western countries who had forsaken a lifestyle of conspicuous consumption and opted for a simpler life on the land certainly seemed happier than their counterparts still preoccupied with acquiring more "stuff."

Less Izmore was a good example. Less was a former bank executive whose previous legal name was Joseph Ciccilone. Less had walked away from a six-figure salary and high-power job in 1988 and started a small commune (somewhat illegally) on Crown land nobody seemed to be using in the middle of the province. The British Columbia government had taken Less and his followers to court multiple times since then (usually when multinational corporations expressed interest in logging the land or fracking for shale gas.) Every two or three years through the 80s and 90s and 00s, some intrepid reporter would visit the commune and do a story on the "crazy hippies." The reporters were not allowed to use video cameras, recorders, still cameras or bring any other newfangled devices such as cell phones with them during their visit. The frequency of recent visits had gone up significantly in direct correlation to the rapidly plummeting economy.

"Crazy hippies, yes. They used to call us that," Less laughed to the reporter. "Tell me honestly, young lady—do we look crazy to you?" Less had been walking with the reporter, KT Burfitt from the *Vancouver Sun*, through their self-sufficient community for the past forty-five minutes. "We raise all our own food here with no chemicals or petroleum-based fertilizers or pesticides. We make everything we need—our clothing from hemp, fur and wool, our tools from wood and repurposed metal and what Mother Earth provides us. We made all our buildings and shelter from natural sustainable materials. Children of all ages are encouraged to attend our community school as often as they like. Our community has zero unemployment . We are all incredibly wealthy, and yet none of us has a single penny or declares ownership of any personal possessions." They stopped by a cabin where two men were carding wool and three women were knitting socks.

"Folks, this bright young button is KT. She's a reporter from Vancouver, but don't hold that against her," Less joked.

"Those socks look wonderfully warm," KT said to the youngest of the ladies.

"Hi, KT. My name is June." June shyly offered a hand to KT and shook it briefly, but then pulled her in for a hug and a kiss on both cheeks. "These socks? Well, they aren't a fashion statement, but they will keep your feet warm and dry. Winter is coming in a few months." June began sorting through handmade baskets of socks. "Size seven work for you?" KT nodded, and June tossed her a pair of thick grey socks. KT was reaching in her purse, but June stopped her by gently grabbing her hand and shaking her head.

The Mouse Who Poked an Elephant * 99

"I feel like I should give you something for these," KT said, blushing.

"Don't be silly," June replied cheerfully. "We have no need of money here, and we are happy to have only the gift of your friendship and company." A bell began to ring from somewhere nearby. "Less, can KT join us for lunch?"

"I'll be disappointed if she doesn't," said Less, holding out two bent arms to escort the girls.

Lunch was served in a long log cookhouse which KT learned also served as a meeting hall, auditorium, dorm, house of worship and gymnasium, among other things. There was a buffet set up at the front of the room, where about twenty people were filling up glazed clay plates. KT followed Less in line, and aided by a menu description from those around her, helped herself to:

- a green salad with dandelions, kale, cranberries, goat cheese, and heirloom grape tomatoes;
- a small piece of cedar-planked salmon with capers;
- some vegan curry with sweet potatoes, lentils, yogurt and wild rice;
- some truly amazing moose ribs; and
- the freshest stir fried snow peas on the planet.

Lunch was a noisy cheerful affair, with everyone seated on benches at four long trestle tables. KT looked around and observed the crowd as she ate. Everybody seemed quite happy and healthy. Genuine laughter and comradeship abounded; it seemed to her like a big happy family. She realized halfway through her meal that she had been truly ravenous, and that this food was remarkable: Michelin Star without the pretentious bullshit remarkable.

"Less? How many people live here?" KT asked as they chatted over chai tea and chicory coffee.

"Hmm…that's a good question for Svanica." Less flagged down a tough-looking girl with spiky hair. "Swan, this is KT. She's wondering how many people live here."

"Hi, KT. Well, we had two hundred and fifty plates set on the buffet table, and I see six left, so…244. That numbers been steady for the past few days, but it fluctuates—oops, excuse me." Swan hustled up to the buffet table to give instructions to a team of people who were returning plates to the scullery

June and the wool sock crew excused themselves, as well, leaving KT with Less in a rapidly emptying mess hall. It all seemed well choreographed. Everyone knew where to go and what to do without anyone appearing to be in charge.

"Swan, can you give KT a tour of the kitchen and pantry?" Without waiting for a response, Less gave them both a quick peck on the cheek.

"Don't worry KT, I'll come back for you," Less promised as he walked backwards toward the door. "We are training a new team of oxen for ploughing. I want to see how they are coming along."

"All right KT, let's not go in the kitchen empty-handed." Swan grabbed one handle of a large basket of dirty dishes, and motioned for KT to take the other side. "One, two, three and lift. Here we go." Swan and KT put the basket by a similar pile of dishes, where two skinny teenage boys and a middle-aged black lady were washing, rinsing and stacking the dishes and cutlery from lunch.

The Mouse Who Poked an Elephant * 101

"So KT—" Swan was briskly efficient, walking and talking in a no nonsense way "—it all starts by the back door. As we bring in our food, depending on what we are receiving, we have separate storerooms." KT opened door number one. "For example, here are all our dry goods—cereals, dry legumes, grains, rice, chicory, pickled and preserved vegetables and so on." Swan paused to count some burlap sacks of oats, and made a quick note on a blackboard by the door.

"This is our dairy fridge—cheese, butter, milk, yogurt." The room was built like a vault with thick adobe walls and a gravel floor. They walked past shelves with rows of delicious smelling cheese wrapped in rough wax cloth, then by stainless steel jugs of milk. "Swan, how do you keep this room cold? I mean is it electric or…?"

Swan laughed. "No, honey, we don't need electricity." She crouched down and brushed away some straw from a large block which was under each shelf. "Look here. See this ice? In the winter, when the lake freezes up, we cut these blocks of ice with a saw and store them in our ice house by the lake. Each block of ice will last three to four weeks here in the coolers, during the summer. The straw just helps to keep it cold. Then, as it cools off in autumn, we can open the wall vents—these flaps—a crack to let in colder outside air." Swan paused to check a thermometer by the door and wrote "4" on a blackboard that tracked the cooler temperature twice daily.

Swan paused by door number three. "KT, are you vegan?" When KT shook her head, Swan opened the door to reveal the meat locker. It was built much like the dairy cooler, with thick walls and beams along the ceiling. Now KT understood the vegan question. From the beams various animals and meats were hanging from hooks, or resting in trays lined with brown waxed paper. Swan handed KT a piece of paper on a cedar shingle, and a pencil. "I'll count it, you write it down."

"Three front and two hind quarters of beef?"

"Check."

"Sixty pounds salt beef?"

"Check."

"Eleven pounds beef cheek?"

"Check."

"Four pickled beef tongues?"

"Ewwwww."

"I know, it looks gross, but it's delicious."

"Check."

"One hind quarter moose?"

"Check."

"Two deer?"

"Awwwwwww."

Stern look from Swan. "Check."

"Six goats?"

"Check."

"Four pigs?"

"Check."

"Six slabs bacon?"

"Mmmm...bacon. Check."

"Eight—no, nine geese?"

"Check."

"Twelve wild turkeys?"

"Check."

The Mouse Who Poked an Elephant ⋆ 103

And so on. The meat locker was forty feet by twenty feet, and impeccably well organized and very clean.

"Well, thank you for saying so, KT. It is a team effort," Swan replied.

They went next to the root cellar: potatoes, squashes of all sorts, cabbages, onions, carrots, pumpkins. Then on to the spice room: sage, savory, dried peppers, wild ginger, juniper berry, cattail root and numerous other spices KT couldn't identify. And finally they hit the bakeshop, where an older deaf Indigenous lady and a young girl gave them scones—right out of the stone oven, dripping with butter and fresh honey. "Oh my heavens, these are amazing." KT hugged both the bakers. "I would be ginormous if I lived here. The food is so crazy good."

Swan shook her head at KT's remark. "Most people who come here from the outside look smaller, or should I say, fitter, after a couple of months.

KT looked doubtful. "But don't people eat more because the food is so good?"

"We may eat more, but it's all real food—there's no additives, or preservatives, or fillers, so the food is better for us. Don't forget—we do all of our chores with people power. To make these scones we ploughed the field, planted, weeded and harvested this wheat, and ground the grain all by hand. A lot of us say it's the sweat that gives the food its flavour."

Swan gestured to a stone millstone that looked ominously heavy. "We are burning more calories every day than someone who drives to work, sits in an office all day, then turns into a couch potato at night in front of a TV or compu—" Swan stopped abruptly as she saw that

KT was blushing. "I'm sorry, KT, I didn't mean to hurt your feelings."

KT waved off the apology, still blushing a bit, but also laughing through it. "I always like to hear the truth, even if it hurts a little. You just described my workweek very accurately."

Awkward.

But just for a second. Less bounced in from a side door, a little out of breath. "KT, do you like baby goats?" Without waiting for an answer, he was already halfway out the door again. "'Cause if you follow me, you can see one being born. Let's go."

"You should go with her, Susanna. See the miracle of birth," Swan said to the younger girl. "I'll help finish up here."

Susanna took KT by the hand and they ran after Less, who was going up a path that led to a pasture. There were about twenty other people leaning quietly on a rail fence. The obviously very pregnant mama goat was lying on her side, in a separate pen, breathing heavily about twenty-five metres from the fence. There were other goats and sheep scattered around the pasture

"We are just gonna hang back here quietly," Less explained in hushed tones. "KT, this is Erica. She's our shepherd and resident midwife—this week. She can explain what's going on to you and Susanna."

"Hey, KT. Hey, Susanna—you been killing it in the bakeshop, girl!" Erica high-fived Susanna's free hand. KT realized that Susanna wasn't going to let her hand go anytime soon.

The Mouse Who Poked an Elephant * 105

"So, this is a seven-year-old Nubian nanny goat named Miss MilksaLot. She's been in labour about two hours now, and things should move along pretty quickly from here on in." Almost as if on cue, Miss MilksaLot rose awkwardly to her feet, revealing a very dilated cervix. Susanna's eyes were big as saucers. The goat grunted and pushed, and a dark watery bag revealed itself in a minute or two.

"Is she pooping?" Susanna asked Erica quietly.

"No, honey. There's a baby goat—a kid—inside that bag. That bag is called an amniotic sac." As they watched, Miss MilksaLot continued to push and the watery sac and the baby goat inside it continued to move out of Momma and toward the ground.

KT noticed Susanna's grip was tightening on her hand. "Can you see the kid now, Susanna?" Erica asked. "Pretty cool, eh?

Susanna nodded "Yeah" to Erica, but whispered "Pretty gross" to KT. The baby goat—still in its watery amniotic sac—was coming out front hooves first. "Textbook," Erica said. The people watching the birth could now see hooves, head and the front half of the kid. With a sudden watery *sploosh,* the sac burst open like a water balloon. About one minute later, Miss MilksaLot successfully delivered her seventh healthy kid.

"Seventh for now—there might be one or two more in there. She had twins as a three-year-old, a stillborn doe from a breech birth as a four-year-old, and healthy twins as a five and six-year-old," Erica was explaining to the crowd, reading from and making notes in a book bound in leather.

"What's all that gross stuff coming out of her now?" Susanna asked.

"That's afterbirth, or the placenta," Erica explained.

"Can this get any grosser?" Susanna wanted to know. Everybody chuckled, but her question was answered in several minutes when Miss MilksaLot began to eat the placenta.

"Ewwwwww. Okay, that does it—I am never, ever havin' a baby," Susanna declared defiantly.

That makes two of us, KT was thinking.

"Let's go help this momma and baby, you two," Erica said, opening a gate in the fence (hoping to reduce the trauma and drama for Susanna and KT). She passed Susanna a rough towel, and handed KT a wooden bucket of warm water, to which she added some honey. They approached Miss MilksaLot slowly and quietly.

Erica spoke in very soft tones. "KT, very slowly, put that bucket of water by our new mother's nose please. The honey will help her regain some strength, and she's bound to be thirsty."

"Susanna, now that nanny goat is drinking, sit over there—that's it—put that towel in your lap, and let's look at this kid." Erica scooped up the tiny goat efficiently and placed it in the towel. "Now, use that towel to dry and warm up our new baby."

"It's all bloody and slippery." Susanna giggled with a mixture of revulsion and happiness, as the kid tried to suckle at her fingers. While the nanny drank and the kid was being cleaned up, two older gentlemen quietly rolled in with a wheelbarrow, rake and shovel. Erica couldn't help but notice that all the tools were handmade—the wheelbarrow had a spoked wooden wheel banded in steel, and the rake and shovel were crudely forged with peeled handles that were clearly branches of trees a few years ago. They scooped up the afterbirth and left the pasture via another gate. Erica could see that KT looked puzzled.

"Isn't it normal for anim—"

"For animals to eat their afterbirth?" Erica finished the question. "Yes and no. Lots of animals do it, but the placenta for these goats is like a tough cellophane bag, and we have learned from experience that some mothers can choke on it. Also, if we leave it here, the smell will attract coyotes or wolves." Erica was wiping the nanny's hind quarters with a damp towel. "Okay, let's see—the nanny and kid are clean and healthy. We have one thing left to do. Susanna, what are we going to call our new baby goat?"

Susanna looked surprised and pleased. "Is it a boy or girl?" she asked thoughtfully.

"You tell us. Flip it over on its back," Erica shot back. "Don't worry, they are tough—you won't hurt it. Now, is that a penis or vagina?

"A penis!" Susanna shouted.

"So what will you call this little billy goat?"

"Billy. The. Kid," Susanna said emphatically. All three girls agreed this was a good choice.

"All right, let's leave these two goats alone." Susanna reluctantly returned Billy to Miss MilksaLot, who nuzzled the kid with her nose and tongue. The girls were backing away slowly as Billy the Kid began to stand on the shakiest legs since Bambi. The few people still watching by the fence applauded politely for all four girls and the new kid.

The two older men who had been on wheelbarrow duty opened the gate for the three girls. "Oh, hey—KT, this is

Heckle and Jekyll. These guys are trouble," Erica said in a stage whisper to KT, while winking at the two men.

"Howdy, ma'am," they said in unison, doffing their hats to KT.

"Gentlemen," KT replied, pretending not to find the names unusual .

"What did you name our new goat little one?" Heckle (Or was it Jekyll?) asked Susanna.

"Billy. The. Kid," Susanna said proudly, "'cause he has a penis, so he's a boy." Susanna picked some small wildflowers for the group as she spoke. *Edelweiss? Pansies?* KT couldn't place them.

Susanna passed one tiny flower to each person present, and then ran back toward the bakeshop with the fearless abandon one only sees in young people.

"Susanna!" KT hollered after her. "Don't forget to wash your hands." Susanna kept running, but held up her hand in the "OK" symbol. The rest of the people who had been watching the birth began to drift away in twos and threes.

"Speaking of washing up," Erica handed KT a bar of rough soap, and nodded her head toward a pail of water.

"Umm, yeah. The goat was licking my hand a lot," KT replied, beginning to lather up.

"Sure, goats do that a lot –it's their way of welcoming you to their flock," said Heckle. "So it's always a good idea to wash up after working with any livestock."

"Especially since goats lick their ass every thirty seconds or so," added Jeckyll.

"Man, I wish I could do that," Heckle stated dreamily into space, leaning on a shovel.

"Don't try it, Heckle. 'Member Uncle Cletus?"

"Sure. What about him?"

"Well, he tried to lick a goat's ass a few years ago, and the goat kicked him in the head."

KT looked at Erica, who just rolled her eyes. "KT, I can make them stop if you want."

"KT held up both hands by her shoulders. "It's okay. I have three brothers."

Heckle and Jekyll took this as approval to continue.

"I don't wanna lick a goat's ass, you pervert," Heckle stated indignantly, grabbing Jekyll's hat and hitting him with it. He lowered his voice, and put his arm around Jekyll's shoulder as if sharing a state secret with a co-conspirator. "I was just saying that I wish I could lick *my* ass."

"Don't try that either, Heckle. 'Member Uncle Festus?"

"Sure, but I haven't seen him for a long time."

"Mmm-hmm. That's just my point," Jekyll explained. "Uncle Festus tried to lick his own ass, and we found him curled up behind the woodstove last February with a broken neck."

KT couldn't help herself from snorting out a laugh.

Erica shook her head. "KT, don't encourage them. They're awful."

Heckle and Jekyll tipped their hats at the girls, picked up their tools and wordlessly headed down the hill away from the pasture toward a barn.

Erica passed KT a rough towel to dry her hands. "KT, I'm sorry if they offended you. We have some…eccentric people here."

"It's all good, girl. Like I said, I have three brothers, and I work in a newsroom."

"Alrighty, then. I want to show you the rest of our animals and some of the farm. Grab that bucket and we'll put it here by the pump."

As they walked, Erica provided a very animated description of what they were seeing. She pointed out that there were seventeen other nanny goats and forty-seven ewes in the same pasture as Miss MilksaLot. There were two larger billy goats used for breeding—a Nubian and a Boer—in the same pasture, "but fenced off separately so they don't get after the girls during lambing and kidding season."

Skirting the field they had just left, they cut through a field of newly planted rye. "This was pasture two years ago. Last year we grew hemp on it. By always rotating what crops we grow and what we use the land for we can keep the soil healthy." Erica pointed to a field on their left. "That field over there was just planted with barley, and we'll plant potatoes in that piece beside it next week."

They paused at the top of the hill, and turned back to look at where they had been. "We call this spot 'Inspiration Point.'" Erica said, twirling in a slow 360. There was a stone fire pit with two rows of wooden benches. "From here you can see the whole valley, and SimpleTown."

"I'm sorry. Did I hear you right?" KT asked. "The community is called SimpleTown?"

"Yeah, that's how most of us Simpletons refer to it." Erica laughed at KT's reaction. "You mean Less didn't tell you we are Simpletons?"

"Why Simpletons?" KT sputtered. " I mean isn't that term a bit...um..."

"Derogatory?" Erica interrupted, smiling. "No, not to us. It's a term of endearment. Sit. I'll explain." Erica gestured at the closest bench, and pulled a joint of her shirt pocket before sitting beside KT. She lit the joint expertly with a rough wooden match, and took a few hauls on it before offering it to KT.

"N-no thanks," KT stuttered, blushing. "I haven't done that since high school."

"'S all good." Erica replied, shrugging good naturedly. "So, I was saying, we 'Simpletons' call ourselves that with pride."

"Look, most of us are here because we believe the Western or 'developed' world is getting too complicated. Too many machines, too many possessions, too many distractions, too much to do, racing from crisis to crisis day after day just to accumulate more worthless shit? What we do here is just the opposite—no machines, no possessions, no distractions. We just live simply. Everything we do—the farming, the buildings, the way we live our lives is in its simplest form, so it keeps us all just busy enough. We aren't all caught up with trying to get more 'stuff.'"

Erica took another long, slow, deep, delicious toke, held her breath, and offered it to KT. "It's really good shit, man," she intoned in her best Tommy Chong voice. KT couldn't help but laugh, and took a few timid puffs. The two girls sat, quietly smoking for a couple minutes.

Looking back down the hill, KT could make out the main meeting hall, the various shared dormitory style living quarters, barns of various sizes...*a greenhouse? And some teepees?* The fields they had just passed through looked like a fuzzy patchwork quilt. *She wasn't kidding—that dope was crazy good. I haven't felt this relaxed in a long... Ever.*

"How long have you been here Erica? KT asked softly.

"Hmm. Almost two years. I tried to escape my old life earlier, but it's hard to take that first step and walk away from everything and everybody." Erica stretched like a contented cat. "I was pretty unhappy back in the rat race, and finally found the courage to get away from all that and turn my life around."

"And what did you used to do…back out there?" KT gestured over the horizon. "I mean, if you don't mind talking about it."

"I don't mind. But I'll give you the condensed version. The whole story is too long, too sad and pretty boring. So, my dad's sperm met my mom's egg, then I grew up in Montreal, and spent my summers with my grandparents at their farm near Lac Champlain. That's where I learned to love places like this." Erica stopped for a moment to pick a long stem of grass and began to chew on it.

"After high school I attended university in Laval. I majored in corporate law and graduated in the top 5 per cent of my class. I then moved to Toronto and articled with a large petro chemical firm, who—for my safety—must remain nameless. They paid me a lot of money to ensure that they never got in trouble for their transgressions, which were legion. I passed the bar on my first attempt, and received multiple promotions and raises over the next four years. I had a beautiful condo, a hot car, a hot, hunky, successful boyfriend and a big expense account. By 'normal' standards I should have been happy." Erica shook her head sadly, and threw the grass stem over her shoulder.

Erica's voice became harder, colder. "But I wasn't happy, KT. I hated my job, because I had to lie to people when my company bent or broke the law; which was often, so I lied a lot. The products my company made were generating tremendous profits to shareholders, but killing poor people and destroying the environment. After four years of ten to twelve-hour days on a perpetual treadmill fuelled by lies and deception I was ready to leave—to run away—to pile up all my useless shit in one big steaming shit pile in my condo and pour gas on it, and light it on fire." Erica was standing now, rocking from side to side, eyes closed. She shook her head as if to clear her thoughts.

Erica's voice lost its edge. "My boyfriend finally convinced me to leave," she said calmly.

"Oh, cool. Is he here, as well?" KT chirped, hoping to lighten the mood.

"Oh, no, no. I meant to say he convinced me to leave when I came home early from work one day and caught him sodomizing a seventeen-year-old boy on our couch." Suddenly it got really quiet. Somewhere in the distance KT could hear goats bleating and frogs peeping.

Erica giggled happily and then continued. "I didn't say anything. I closed the door and never looked back. I'm really grateful to him for giving me the inspiration to finally sever my ties with a life I hated and making this change. I had visited this commune five years ago, and always wanted to come back and live here. I had a trustee sell all my stuff and donated a considerable sum of money to charitable organizations. I kept some money put aside in case I ever want to go back, but I don't think I ever will." Erica sighed, and looked surprisingly happy.

She crouched down and grabbed KT's hands. "Can you keep a secret? Girl to girl?"

"Um, sure I can."

"You really can't tell anybody."

"I won't. I promise."

"Okay. That day when I came home and caught my boyfriend sodomizing a boy half my age? Well, I may have taken one or two photos of that before I left. And somehow those photos may have been sent to a private investigator who may have told me that the boy in question was an underage male prostitute. And then somehow the story got leaked to the police, and then when the police seemed reluctant to investigate an elected member of Parliament in Stephen Sharpe's Conservative Cabinet, it got leaked to the press, which embarrassed the police into action. Any of this sound familiar?" Erica laughed at KT's reaction.

"Oh, my God," KT squealed. "You were dating John Giacomo? He was so hot and then so… yucky…but he's… he's in prison now, and had to resign as an MP. That was, like, the biggest story of 2014. He was on a short list to lead the party and—oh, my God."

Erica stood up with a wry smile. "Do you want to hear the best part?"

"Of course. Spill."

"I may have had some—let's call them acquaintances—check into the young man in question. I was hopeful that he could be saved from himself and the sort of people who used those services. Because he was a minor at the time of the incident, his identity had been protected throughout the trial. I had my friends arrange for him to be cleaned up and dried out. He was pretty new to the streets and still surprisingly free of any diseases." Erica sat down again and leaned back with her eyes closed.

KT was still trying to absorb that information when Erica spoke again. Quietly and softly, almost as if she were speaking to herself. "That boy is now in one of the safest places I know."

KT looked puzzled. "He's here, KT. He's safe with us. And he loves it here." Erica wiped away some happy tears and hugged KT.

Down in the valley, a bell started ringing. Erica jumped up. "Don't forget what I said, KT—you can't tell another soul that story. If I can get an elected official sent to prison…." She let her voice trail off. Sometimes what was unsaid could be scarier than the spoken threat. "Come on. That bell is saying it's supper time. Let's introduce you to some more of our family."

As they began to walk, a group of four men and three girls came out of the woods behind them. They whistled at Erica and KT who stopped and waited for them. Two of the men were carrying a big two-handled saw, and everybody else had an axe or water jug or some kind of handmade tool that looked like a museum piecce.

"You must be KT. Less told us that we should expect a visitor." The lady who spoke and shook KT's hand enthusiastically looked like she had some significant decades of experience as a hippie chick. Lean muscle, very tanned, 1970s hair, complete with peasant dress and flower necklace. "I'm Rainbow. This here is MoonBeam and ThunderCloud." KT was shaking each hand in turn when the group broke out laughing. *What's so funny?*

"KT, I apologize," Rainbow was explaining. "I'm just messin' with you. I desperately wanted to be called Rainbow back in the day, but that ship sailed long ago. My name is Dorothy Williams. This is my nephew, Noah, and his wife, Ashley." Dorothy prattled on with introductions, and KT shook each hand warmly, while thinking: *Your 1970s hippie commune names were easier to remember.*

"Anyway, don't worry about the names," Noah said. The group was moving back down the hill again. "There's not a test. Here is a more important question. Are you hungry, KT? 'Cause we set a pretty good table here in SimpleTown."

KT grinned. "I shouldn't be hungry, 'cause I ate like a lumberjack at lunch, but…" The group laughed, and KT blushed as she realized she was walking with lumberjacks.

"Don't worry, KT," Dorothy was saying. "It's normal to be hungry out here. It's the fresh air and hard work. And, FYI, I'm a lumberjill, not a lumberjack." Dorothy punched KT good naturedly on the arm, and both girls laughed.

The group joined two lines of people who were washing up for supper. Twin boys, who looked about three years old were standing on two step stools. Each boy manned a wooden pump. Each person washing put their hands under the spout and got one pump to get wet (two if you put your head under the spout), stepped aside to get lathered up, and then stepped back for a pump or two to rinse off.

KT followed along with Erica and Dorothy and the gang. The dining hall was buzzing with people chatting and eating. The buffet line seemed even bigger than at lunch.

There were five different salads to pick from, and a hearty bean soup.

There were roasted sweet potatoes, and scalloped potatoes, and peas and carrots, and rainbow Swiss chard and sauteed zucchini.

There was baked trout, and curried goat with roasted barley.

There were three types of cheese, and a bread board, and Susanna's scones, served by Susanna herself. She beamed when she saw KT, and blushed proudly at the compliments being paid to her skills as a baker.

The biggest and most delicious looking baked ham KT had ever seen was being sliced to order by a very large black man in a leather apron. "Slide your plate on in here, KT," he said with a warm grin wrapped up in a soft southern drawl. "We smoked this here ham for three weeks over a slow maple and applewood fire. Mmmmm- mmmmm!" He put a generous slice on KT's already heaping plate.

"Thank you. Everything looks so delicious," she replied.

KT sat with Erica and Dorothy and Noah and Ashley and the lumberjacks and Jills. As they ate and chatted, she noticed people she had met earlier in the day. Less was talking animatedly with a group of teens, the wool sock gang were laughing with Heckle and Jekyll and some of the people who had been watching the birth of Billy the Kid. The big man who had been slicing the ham sat down to join KT, along with Susanna and the older lady from the bakeshop.

"Name's Tiny, KT. Tiny Jackson." Her hand disappeared in his massive paw as he shook it warmly. "That's my girlfriend, Chevonne," he continued, reaching across the table to pat Chevonne's hand. Chevonne nodded and winked at KT. "And I believe you met Susanna earlier this afternoon." He tickled the young girl under the chin. "Now 'scuse me while I pay some attention to this here ham."

The chatter subsided quickly as the two young twin boys who had been on water pump duty climbed the steps to a stage just left of the buffet tables. They were joined by a girl barely in her teens who carried a stool and a guitar. She sat on the stool, and began to play a simple tune. While she played, each boy peeled and started eating a banana, while acting like monkeys. When they were done eating, the two boys joined in with the girl singing "Apples and Bananas."

The crowd applauded politely as they finished. The girl left the stage quietly, but the two boys hammed it up with multiple bows and a double moon. That got their mother up, who cleared them off the stage while blushing and apologizing.

Next a young man about fifteen years old took the stage. "Thank you, Gabriel, Gideon and Emily. Just a quick word about that song—we've been able to grow apples here for quite a while, but Gabriel and Gideon had their first banana today from our greenhouse,"

The young man paused politely and waited for the applause and whistles to die down. "We just want to say thanks to Susan and Jimbo for encouraging us to build the greenhouse. It's gonna extend both our growing season, and the variety of fruits and vegetable we can grow."

The Simpletons whistled and cheered until Susan and Jimbo stood and acknowledged them.

"Glass is one of the few things we aren't making ourselves—yet," Erica explained to KT. "Jimbo used to run a demolition firm in Vancouver, so he is able to get glass panels and old windows donated to SimpleTown for our buildings."

Heckle and Jekyll took the stage next. "Work draw, ladies and gentlemen," Heckle—*Or was it Jekyll?*—wheeled in a big board.

"See, KT?" Tiny pointed to the board, speaking quietly. "Across the top of the board are the general work locations and teams—Barns, Kitchen Prep, Scullery, Gardens, Pastures, Construction, Laundry, Housekeeping, Childcare."

As KT watched, people came forward and drew their assignments from a box. Each person then showed Heckle or Jekyll what they had drawn, and their name was put on the board. Gideon drew Construction, Gabriel drew Gardens, their Mother drew Barns, Susanna drew Childcare… Erica grabbed KT's hand and they joined the lineup. Erica drew Housekeeping, KT drew Scullery…and the names piled up under the various work assignments.

"Who didn't draw an assignment?" Heckle asked Jekyll.

"You two!" shouted the crowd. Heckle drew Scullery. *Ahhhh, Heckle is the older looking one,* KT realized as his name was written on the board.

"All right Scullery, let's get cracking!" Heckle shouted.

"Go with Heckle. He'll show you what to do," Susanna told KT. Sure enough, Heckle steered her toward a table with a wooden bucket on either side. "KT, people are gonna bring you plates in a minute. If there's food left on the plate that a pig can eat, scrape it in the bucket on the left. If a pig shouldn't eat it, put in the other tub—we'll compost it. Questions?"

"Yes. What can't a pig eat? Won't they eat everything?" KT asked innocently.

Heckle laughed. "Well, now, KT—that's a good question. A pig will indeed eat almost anything and everything, but we don't want them to eat meat—especially pork—or they might get a taste for each other. We also don't let them have onion peels—they can choke on them. Anyway, I'll be right here beside you." Plates were coming in quickly and being dropped off on the table. "Put 'em here after you scrape 'em." Heckle demonstrated by stacking three plates on a tray.

"These plates are pretty clean," KT said after a minute.

"Yep, that's good," Heckle replied with a grin. "We always tell people not to put more on their plates than they can eat. After you've been here a while, you learn not to waste anything. 'Cause we've all learned how hard it is to plant and grow and raise this food."

As Heckle and KT scraped and stacked plates and bowls, a girl and an older lady passed stacks of dishes to a boy and an old man who washed them. Two more people worked sliding the plates into a very hot rinse, then pulling them out with wooden tongs and stacking them on their edge in racks.

After fifteen minutes, KT and Heckle were done scraping. "All right, KT. Come with me and we'll put 'em away." At the other end of the line, plates, cups, cutlery and bowls were air drying in wooden racks built for each purpose.

"Do we dry them with towels, or…?" KT asked.

"No, ma'am—we just let 'em air dry," Heckle explained. "It's more sanitary—that's a really hot rinse. We are just gonna stack the racks one on top of the other." The washers finished up with pots and trays and cooking utensils, which were then hung on hooks.

"What's next?" KT asked the group.

"I think we are pretty much done for tonight," Heckle replied. "You and I could each take a bucket out to the pigs and the compost pile. The rest of these cats we'll see at the show tonight, or tomorrow morning at six thirty." Heckle high-fived the other six members of the scullery team, and the seven of them then circled around KT.

"Group hug," the youngest boy shouted, after which they drifted back out to the main assembly hall.

"Grab that bucket, kiddo, and follow me." Heckle hoisted the smaller bucket destined for compost, and KT grabbed the swill bucket. They walked about two hundred metres to the pig barn, where KT was told eighteen pigs resided. "Who gets the swill bucket, Naomi?" Heckle asked a young girl. Naomi pointed to a pen with a momma pig and nine tiny piglets.

Momma was laying down with suckling piglets, but she got up pretty quick when she saw the swill bucket.

"Just pour all that delicious swill right into that trough, KT," Naomi said. The next few minutes were filled with some pretty enthusiastic eating noises, as the pig feasted on whatever scraps the Simpletons hadn't eaten for supper. While Momma feasted, Naomi reached in and grabbed the smallest piglet and handed it to KT.

"This might be the cutest thing I've ever seen," KT said.

"I can't disagree, " retorted Naomi. "Pigs are the perfect animal—cute, friendly, and, eventually delicious."

KT grimaced at that thought, but Heckle reminded her, "That smoked ham you had tonight? That's this little fellow in eighteen months."

When Momma had licked her trough clean, Naomi held out her hands, and took the piglet back from a reluctant KT.

Heckle led the way out of the pig barn, and dumped the compost bucket on a big pile. "Grab that pitchfork, KT, and fork some of that rotted compost on top of what we just put there." As KT forked, Heckle explained, "Our compost piles are very important to us—you see that steam?"

KT nodded. "That's a healthy sign. A good working pile gets hot as the bacteria works to break down organic matter—turns it back into super soil that we can use to enrich our gardens and put back onto the land."

A bell tolled back in the assembly hall. "C'mon, KT. Showtime!" Heckle grinned. Other Simpletons were walking back to the hall as well. A few folks stood outside smoking some of that delicious BC bud, but most were already back inside the hall.

As they entered, Susanna ran up and grabbed KT's hand. "Enjoy the show KT." Heckle winked at the two girls. "I think Miss Susanna would like you to sit with her."

Candles were lit on the tables, and a curtain was drawn across the stage. Susanna led KT to a table closest the stage, filled with people from three to eighteen years old. Tiny Jackson approached, wheeling a wooden cart laden with mugs. "KT, tonight on tap we have an elderberry wine or a brown ale. Or there's coffee, tea, milk, juice, and water at that table at the back of the hall."

KT took a mug of ale and sipped. "Oh, that's nice." Some of the older kids at the table took wine or ale from the cart. As Tiny wheeled his cart back to the second table, the show began.

The master of ceremonies was a very handsome young man of Japanese extraction, who welcomed KT warmly to SimpleTown's weekly variety show amid polite applause and whistles. The show lasted ninety minutes and included:
- a morality piece featuring animal puppets;
- a barbershop quartet;
- a magic act in which Susanna was cut in half;
- a folk medley with Noah and Ashley playing the saw and wooden bucket drums behind three girl singers;
- a tumbling act featuring most of the kids;
- three achievement awards presented to the weekly winners for inspiration, perspiration and dedication;
- a tug of war with the ten biggest men versus everyone under three feet tall (the short team won); and
- a ladies choir.

Susanna fell asleep in KT's lap during the choir's act. As the crowd cleared out of the hall, Swan and Less noticed her predicament. "If you pick her up, I can show you where she sleeps," Less said as he and Swan each scooped up a sleeping child.

KT followed with Susanna but she was curious. "Should we tell Susanna's parents we are putting her to bed?"

Less and Swan looked at each other and smiled sadly. "Honey, we aren't sure where Susanna's folks are." Swan seemed lost for words. "We're her family now—all of us in this little village."

Less said proudly. "It takes a village to raise…well, you know the rest."

Less held the door for the girls, and Swan pointed to a top bunk in a tiny room dimly lit with a candle. There was a nightdress for Susanna on the pillow. KT lowered the drowsy girl gently into the bunk. She gently pulled Susanna's shirt over her head, and then KT gasped. The little girl's back and chest were criss-crossed with old scars and healed-over burns.

Swan made a "shhh" motion with a finger to her lips. "I'll tell you after," she said quietly to KT. The two girls worked together to pull a nightdress over sleeping arms and head, then covered Susanna up tenderly. "Good night, KT," Susanna mumbled sleepily.

"Good night, sweetheart," KT said, kissing her forehead and doing her best not to cry.

"Follow me," Swan said, going down a long central hall, then turning into another candle lit bedroom with eight bunkbeds. "Welcome to single female headquarters." Swan paused. "If you are still single—that is, if you've already met somebody—we have rendez-vous rooms we can make available." KT shook her head and blushed. Swan pointed to a rough chest of drawers. "Less had your overnight bag put here when you arrived."

"Hey, can we talk about Susanna?" KT interjected quickly.

"Sure, I'll tell you what I know." Swan sat on a bunk, and patted the space beside her. Her voice went cold again. "But understand, if that little girl's story is mentioned in your newspaper, I will hunt you down, and I will cripple you."

These are some passionate people. KT nodded, and took a seat beside Swan.

Over the next five minutes, she heard Susanna's short history of life in SimpleTown. She was found by a neighbouring farmer friendly to the Simpletons in late October wandering a logging road, emaciated, dehydrated, dressed in rags and nearly frozen to death. The farmer was an old bachelor, not fond of town or city folk. He brought Susanna to SimpleTown.

"I was a social worker in another life, KT, so I've seen some horrible cases of abuse, but Susanna's case was…well, the act of a sick person or persons. She didn't speak to anyone for a week. Please don't suggest we should turn Susanna over to child services. I know that system. It's… broken. Most of the people in it mean well, but they are overwhelmed and understaffed and paralyzed by their own bureaucratic regulations. Susanna is safe here. She is terrified that whoever did these…things…to her will find her if she leaves here."

Swan patted KTs leg, and stood up. "It's nine-thirty. There's a fire up the hill, usually some music, some smoke, I can take you up if you like?"

KT shook her head. "I'm tired. Maybe all the fresh air?"

"Uh-huh. Everybody sleeps well here. C'mon, I'll show you the washrooms if you wanna wash up."

KT grabbed a big leather bag of toiletries from her backpack and followed Swan. As they were brushing their teeth in a communal wash space, Erica, June and Dorothy came in.

"Hey, sisters!" Dorothy called out, flashing them a peace sign, and giggling.

"Have you tried that latest batch of Erica's weed?" The girls all looked at each other grinning.

"'Cause I am so hammered right now," Dorothy continued to more laughter.

"Hey, is that a hair dryer?" she asked, quickly pulling it out of KT's toiletry bag and looking in vain for a socket to plug it into. The other girls were really laughing hard now.

"KT, we're laughing with you, girl, not at you," Dorothy said, suddenly serious. "You girls wanna know what I really miss from the outside?"

"Sure. What?" the four chimed in around toothbrushes and washcloths.

"D-cell batteries," Dorothy said wistfully. The other girls looked at each other quizzically.

"What?"

"Yeah. D-cell batteries, " Dorothy continued. "'Cause I snuck a vibrator in here back in 1997, but the batteries only lasted a week." The room exploded in laughter. The kind of laughter that girls sharing a secret sounds like.

I have never slept better than that, KT realized as she stretched to the sound of a crowing rooster. *Hmmm*. Erica and June were still asleep in each other's arms.

The next few days went by quickly for KT. Her scullery duties only took up two hours of her daily time. When not washing dishes, she helped the construction team lift logs for a new dormitory; planted some heritage blue potatoes; weeded some beans, fed chickens and collected eggs; tried to knit; helped stuff hemp cloth mattress bags with fine chopped straw; stacked stones for a rock wall; helped track and corral a runaway highland goat named Rambo; was dragged by a team of oxen while learning how to plough;

bottle-fed a tiny baby pig that wasn't getting enough milk; buried the same baby pig when it died that night; helped skin, gut and dress two sheep; milked a goat; made soap and candles…

All the Simpletons came out to say goodbye the morning KT left. She'd never been hugged by 244 people before. She did a pretty good job of holding herself together till Susanna said goodbye.

Two days later, Less asked for quiet after lunch. "I want you all to meet somebody," he said. "Please help me welcome Miss KT Burfitt to SimpleTown!" Gabriel and Gideon opened the stage curtains to a blushing KT hugging Susanna.

CHAPTER 8.

A Snowball's Chance in Hell

Benjamin, Elijah, Juliette and Danni were meeting with the local organizers of their first rally. They had chosen to tour the country, with rallies in provincial capitals, beginning and ending the tour in Ottawa. There were approximately eighty thousand people on the Parliament grounds.

Three bands had been playing over the last couple hours.

Like a Motorcycle was up first, and they got the crowd jumping.

A Tribe Called Red played next, and crushed it.

The Comically Hep was onstage now. Their frontman, George Downie, was somehow courageously clinging to life and performing. The Hep finished their set and introduced Elijah to a pretty pumped-up crowd.

"Welcome to Ottawa," Elijah shouted out to a rollicking roaring and adoring crowd.

"Welcome to a new beginning for Canada and Canadians." The crowd noise was almost deafening.

"First thing—don't be assholes here today." Laughter, nervous applause and hoots.

"By that I mean, don't wreck shit, and don't fight with people who have opposing views to ours or yours." Bigger roar of approval.

"The Independent People's Party is going to host thirteen more rallies similar to this—one in each provincial or territorial capital over the next few weeks." Rooooaaaaarrrr.

"At each rally, we will identify key platforms that our group proposes to implement if elected."

Roar!

"But first I need to talk about our party's financial situation." The crowd remained subdued this time, and looked at Elijah and each other curiously.

"I'm just messin' witchoo—we don't have any money!" Elijah shouted cheerfully. Hoots and hollers, shrill whistles...

"And we don't need any money!" Roar! "Because we won't need to spend any money to win this election." Ginormous roar. "Because we are not a 'normal' political party." Earth-shaking roar.

"Five key points, people. These are things we will try to do if we are elected as members of this Parliament. Are you ready?" The crowd went nuts.

Elijah lowered his voice a couple decibels. "So, lemme get these points out. Then when I hold up my hand, let's hear you. Try it out." The crowd buzzed a bit expectantly, then exploded when Elijah raised his hand. "Nice."

"Okay, point number one--eliminate political parties." A few people began to cheer, but Elijah hushed them, palms down. "I don't think I raised my hand there, did I?"

"No!" the crowd shouted back as one.

"So, listen. Here is why we want to change the current broken political system. Groupthink mentality by the major political parties is paralyzing most democracies today, including our own here in Canada. Currently, Conservatives must criticize every Liberal idea, and vice versa. To combat the paralysis inflicted by groupthink, the IPP intends to eliminate political parties, including our own after we are elected. This will allow good ideas from individuals to be respectfully debated, and voted on in an effective Parliament."

Elijah raised his voice. "So, point one—eliminate political parties!" He raised a triumphant fist, and the crowd screamed its approval.

"Point number two—establish a maximum four-year term of service for elected persons." The crowd began to buzz a little. "Whoa, whoa, *tabernac*. Let me explain why we want to do this."

Elijah moved from behind the podium to the left corner of the stage. "It's because we currently have a system that rewards professional politicians and the political parties they belong to. The longer an individual or party stays in power, the more favours they owe to the corporations and establishment fat cats who contributed money to their campaign fund, and to their political party."

Elijah returned to the podium at centre stage. "So, point two—we propose that a four-year term will be the maximum period of service for elected office in Canada." He raised his fist and, once again, the crowd screamed its approval.

"Point number three." He paused briefly then shouted angrily, "Tax carbon users and punish polluters!"

The mob didn't care that Elijah hadn't signalled for their approval—they gave it at a deafening level that lasted more than a minute. Elijah quieted the crowd and lowered his voice.

"I hope that most of us here today believe that we have a responsibility to future generations—a responsibility to safeguard this planet, and leave it to our children in better shape than when we were here." Elijah crossed to the right side of the stage, to better engage the massive crowd near the Rideau Canal and Rideau Centre.

"Here's a sad stone-cold fact. Listen. The generation known as the baby boomers lost sight of this responsibility to safeguard our planet."

The crowd was suddenly very quiet as Elijah slowly paced the stage like a Mississippi preacher in a revival tent. "This generation focused on wealth." Pause. "Wealth."

"Industrial growth." Pause. "At any cost." Pause.

"Corporate profit."

"Personal wealth." Pause.

Shouting now, visibly pissed off. "Conspicuous consumption. The accumulation of more *stuff*—bigger, better, faster, newer things. More property, bigger homes, bigger faster cars, bigger faster boats, bigger cottages, smaller, faster, smarter computers, bigger TVs. We no longer make or grow any of the things we consume—we just consume!"

Elijah was on a roll now, shuckin' and jivin', machine-gun delivery.

"The things we have been consuming come from somewhere else, made in sweatshops by people willing to work harder than ourselves for far less pay. The food we eat is being planted and harvested and raised and butchered by brown and yellow people in some other country. For the past twenty years, we haven't cared where it's from as long as it's cheap!" The crowd was buzzing, angry, yet feeling somewhat guilty at the same time.

"And all these 'things' that we think we need to consume can be brought to us consumers in ships and planes and trains and trucks and pipelines." Quietly again. "Because oil and gas are cheap." Elijah gave the crowd a minute to ponder this.

"So if we tax carbon users heavily, by taxing goods that travel great distances heavily, those low-priced goods being brought in from other countries will no longer be so affordable. And Canadian entrepreneurs will realize that we can make things and grow things right here. And Canadians will have jobs again. Simultaneously, we'll be reducing our planet's carbon footprint and reliance on cheap fossil fuels to transport shit all over the world."

Elijah held up three fingers to the assembly. "So that's the reason behind point three. To tax carbon users and punish polluters!" he shouted, fist raised, and the crowd roared on cue.

BBC1 correspondent Eileen Murphy was one of many journalists covering the IPP rally live in Ottawa.

She re-appeared now on BBC viewers screens. "Elijah addressed the crowd for several more minutes. He spoke to two more key points the Independent People's Party intends to implement. He spoke about pulling Canada out of international trade agreements such as the North American Free Trade Agreement and the Trans Pacific Partnership. As a final point, he stated that the IPP would reduce salaries of elected officials by 25 per cent, and reduce the pension payouts to elected officials by 50 per cent."

Malcolm Furness was the host of BBC's international news team. "Eileen, are average Canadian voters taking Elijah and the Independent People's Party seriously?" Malcolm asked.

"Malcolm, the 'average' Canadian has been changed recently by time and circumstance. Five years ago, the 'average' Canadian was easier to identify." The camera panned the crowd as the young reporter responded. There was a diverse range of persons in the crowd: hippies, executives, punks, grandfathers, bikers, priests, geeks, babies, jocks, hobos and prom queens. There were millenials, Gen X and Y, plus young families, middle-aged suburbanites and the elderly." Five years ago, the average Canadian had a job, and their standard of living was among the highest in the world. Five years ago the Canadian economy was very strong, and the national unemployment rate was at 7 per cent. Today, however, collapsed global markets, and reduced demand for exports over the past few years have significantly weakened the Canadian economy. The unemployment rate stands at 15 per cent today. Malcolm, if there is such a thing as an 'average' Canadian, I believe many of them are here today."

"Thank you, Eileen. That was Eileen Murphy from our Ottawa bureau. Our next story tracks the cleanup efforts—or lack thereof—of an oil spill in the Gulf of Mexico…"

Dustin Trudel clicked off the TV. "Sophia, do you need a hand with the kids?" he called out.

"No, baby. I got this. I'll be right down." Dustin Trudel poured two glasses of his wife's favourite wine, and put another log on the fire.

As she entered the room, Sophia closed the door to the salon and spoke quietly. "Dustin, I had a hard time with Eugenie tonight. She was crying because she is being teased by kids in her school saying 'Your dad's a loser' and 'Your dad sucks' and so on. What can we do about this?"

As she spoke, she reclined on the sofa and put her feet in her husband's lap. Dustin began to give his wife a foot rub, and Sophia stretched and meowed like a pussycat.

"Hmm—that's not cool. I'll talk to the teacher and principal and see if they can address the issue. I mean, these kids are either watching the news or listening to their parents. Surely they didn't decide on their own that I suck." *Did they?*

"I suppose that's about all we can do. Hopefully, it won't make it worse…"

"Or I could have our security guys lay a beating on these punks? Do you think that would help?"

Sophia punched her husband's shoulder, giggling. "They're grade one girls. That might be an overreaction."

"Or I could have President Trimp hit their homes with a drone strike…"

"Ewwww—don't even say that creep's name in our house. You know I can't stand 'He Who Can Not Be

Shamed.'" Sophia put down her wine glass. "Wait a minute." Her tone had changed quickly. "Is there something you aren't telling me? Why did you bring up that name?"

"Uhhh—well, I wish now that I had introduced the topic more gracefully…"

"Just tell me already."

"Okay. Here it is. Foreign Affairs is recommending that we have President Trimp and his family in Ottawa for a state visit within the next few—" The PM did not finish speaking before Sophia reacted.

She threw her wine glass across the room, where it shattered on the granite stones above the fireplace. She quickly removed her feet from Dustin's lap, and stood up, eyes blazing.

"Well, good luck with that Mister Prime Minister. I will *not* be here to play the role of dutiful wife. I assure you that the kids and I will be not be in this country during that visit." Sophia had always been strong-willed, but this was a little over-the-top even for her. She stormed out of the room and slammed the door, leaving the prime minister alone with his thoughts. For a second at least.

Security rapped at the door. A very large Pakistani RCMP officer in plainclothes appeared. "Sir, is everything all right?" he asked quietly.

"Yes, thank you Lateef. We just dropped a glass of wine…and had a bit of a disagreement."

"Sir, there is no need to be explaining anything to me. I have been married for some eleven years now." He rolled his eyes as if to indicate he understood the heavy burden of marriage. "I'll get Monique. Sir, we can clean that up in no time at all." The officer disappeared quietly, and appeared again with Monique, who bore a bucket, dustpan and broom.

"My apologies to both of you for this." Both Monique and Lateef assured the PM no apology was necessary, "It's only a broken wine glass" and so on. Dustin Trudel was clearly embarrassed.

"Monique, I think maybe I'll sleep in the spare bedroom by the office tonight. Again, thank you both, and good night."

CHAPTER 9.

It Still Seems Unlikely

"Dude, why do you live here? I mean look at this place—it's so…flat."

"Well, home skillet, I live here 'cause there were jobs here until recently, and 'cause we got land from Sherry's parents, and built a house. And Sherry has a job here. But choowanna know my favourite reason for living here?"

"Sure, man, spill. And quit bogartin' that joint."

"Well, if your dog runs away here, you can watch it for three days." All three occupants of the van laughed. The joke wasn't that funny, but the dope was.

"Oh, dude. By the way, nobody says 'home skillet' anymore. That was over in 2006. Living out here in the badlands is reducing your coolness level to near zero."

"Yeah- well - that's what happens. I'm married with children. I'm not gonna be current again till my kids are in grade five."

The van went quiet for a minute. The temperature was nearing thirty-four degrees Celsius in Canada's breadbasket. Two figures appeared as a shimmery blur on a blacktop horizon. The land was so flat, it was hard to tell if they were five kilometres away, or one, or ten…

"Hey, should I pick up these hitch-hikers?" the driver asked his passengers as they got closer. "We got four empty seats in the van."

"Dude—no way. Who hitch-hikes anymore? They're prob'ly axe-murdering rapists who just escaped from a lunatic asylum or…hey—what the hell? Slow down—look at his sign." A slender black man was holding a cardboard sign that read:

ELIJAH
RALLY
REGINA

"Dude, stop—that's Elijah, the guy from TV," the passenger cackled, jumping up and down in his seat like a frog dropped onto a hot griddle. The driver braked hard, pulled over in a cloud of dust, and backed up to the two hitch-hikers.

"Hey, thanks for stopping," Elijah said with a grin.

"No problem. We are going right into Regina," the driver said. "I'm Trevor and that's T-Bone and Lumpy."

Lumpy slid over the middle seat into the back seat of the minivan. "Here, you guys can have the middle seats. And pass me those backpacks." Lumpy was having a hard time not staring at the very pretty Indigenous girl Elijah was with.

"Nice to meet you. Cheers, Lumpy. This is Danni, and I'm—"

"Dude, you're Elijah. You don't gotta tell us—we're super crazy fans of your show," T-Bone gushed. "Please tell me you are gonna be back for season five? But, you're trying to be a politician? And why are you hitch-hiking in the middle of Saskatchewan? Don't TV stars make lotsa money? Enuff to buy a nice car? And couldn't you just fly everywhere you need to go anyways?

"Well, those are all good questions." Elijah laughed. Danni handed Elijah a half full refillable water bottle, and he drained it before answering. "Thanks, Danni. So, T-Bone—yes, I am running as an Independent candidate in the upcoming election. If I get elected as an MP, then I'm gonna take some time away from television. Television does pay well, but I don't own a car 'cause I don't need a car. And I don't like to fly unless I have to because it's needlessly hard on the environment. When I have time, I like to take a bus, or, like today, just hitch-hike, or use Uber."

"But, dude, politics is so boring. It's all old guys in suits using big words nobody understands. And no matter what they say, nothin' ever changes. That's why a lot of people don't even vote. You are walking away from a cool TV job to argue with old guys in suits?" Lumpy seemed amazed that anyone would consider such a possibility.

"Well, if this was 1985 you would be absolutely correct," Danni jumped in enthusiastically. "Sure, thirty years ago politicians were all old white guys. And for a long time, they made decisions that they thought would help Canadians—especially old white Canadians—be successful. But the world is changing quickly, and I think people of all ages should have a voice in our future. If we leave all of our political decisions to white men over sixty, then, of course they are going to pass laws that benefit old white people. But there are a lot of young candidates—like myself, for example—running in this election. We're hopeful that we can make politics interesting again."

"Ahhhh, you're the girl! Danni Grey Eyes. I read about you last week. These boys are visiting from Hamiliton. Tell them where you're running." Trevor smiled at her in the rear-view mirror.

"DMC."

Lumpy and T-Bone looked lost. "The proper name for the riding is Desnethe-Missinippi-Churchill River, so you can see why we shorten it to DMC," Danni shared.

"What do you do back in DMC when you're not running to be a member of Parliament?" T-Bone questioned.

"I'm the Chief of the Mistawasis First Nation. And I love what I'm doing now, but I think I can bring some good ideas to Ottawa if I'm elected."

Elijah was busy texting as Danni enlightened her new friends on the challenges and opportunities that Saskatchewan, Canada and First Nations Peoples faced/offered.

"Elijah, where do you need to go?" Trevor asked, as exit signs for Regina began to appear.

"Well, there's a rally this afternoon at the legislative building, but we don't want to take you out of your way…"

"'S all good, my man. Boys, we are heading for a rally!" T-Bone and Lumpy hooted and yee-hawed. "Oops—I should let my wife know, though."

Trevor pressed a button on the steering wheel, and an interactive panel lit up on the dash. "Robot, call Sherry's cell phone," he commanded in an imperial voice.

"Calling Sherry's cell phone," the robot responded woodenly.

"It's not really a robot," Lumpy whispered seriously to Danni, as he passed her a joint. She took a small hit and giggled as the phone rang.

"Hey, baby, what's up?"

"Hey, girl, hey. You're on speakerphone," Trevor said excitedly. "And you won't believe who is in the van with me."

"Is it Lumpy and T-Bone?"

"Yeah, they're here"

"Hi, Sherry," the boys chimed in.

"Hi, knuckleheads," Sherry responded, in that tired voice that girls reserve for old friends of husbands who are barely tolerated when visiting occasionally, drinking too much and pissing on the floor instead of in the toilet.

Trevor silenced them imperiously with a wave. "So, you'll never guess who else is with us."

"Is it Jesus?"

"No."

"Is it Adolf Hitler?"

"No."

"Then you are right. I will never guess who it is, so just tell me already."

"It's Elijah."

"You do *not* have Elijah in our minivan with Beavis and Butthead." Sherry sounded unconvinced. Lumpy and T-Bone were grinning. They'd been called worse.

The Mouse Who Poked an Elephant * 143

"We do. And we are taking him and a friend of his called Danni to a political rally in Wascana Park—you know, at the legislative building."

"I don't believe you."

"Hi, Sherry," Elijah jumped in. "Trevor is telling you the truth. This is Elijah. I was up at Mistawasis visiting a friend and touring some of the reserves. Trevor picked us up a few minutes ago."

"Oh. My. Gawd. It is you—I'd know that voice anywhere," Sherry screeched over the speakerphone. Trevor knocked the volume down a bit.

"So, Listen. I'm a ginormous fan. Could you do me a solid please and autograph the dashboard of our van in big letters? There's a Sharpie in the glove compartment. Could you please sign it "To Sherry and Trevor, love Elijah?" And then get a picture with you and Trevor and the autograph?"

"Sure thing, Sherry. Here comes Trevor back on…"

The Regina Rally for IPP was a tremendous success. Each rally had become a bigger thing, with musicians and artists joining the movement. After the first rally in Ottawa, Elijah appeared in each provincial capital: Toronto, Quebec, Fredericton, Halifax, Charlottetown and St John's. Victoria was next, followed by Edmonton. From Edmonton, he had gone north to Whitehorse, Yellowknife and Iqaluit, then back south to Winnipeg. Regina was the final stop. Elijah had taken only five flights while crisscrossing Canada. He flew from St John's, Newfoundland, to Victoria, then from Edmonton to the three northern territorial capitals, and back to Winnipeg.

During the campaign, he insisted that each person running under the IPP banner list all their expenses on the party's website. Elijah's campaign expenses were $6,317.11 with three days left before the election. He included a detailed itinerary, such as "Hitchhiked from Mistawasis to Regina with Danni from DMC. Got a ride with Trevor Cluett, Lumpy Halerewich and T-Bone Brown. Much thanks for the company, for keeping our costs low, and our environmental footprint lower."

Elijah's website listed and thanked every person who had helped him and his team out during the campaign. It included people who had done laundry for him and his companions, who fed them, who provided them with sleeping quarters and showers, who provided IT support, and transportation. It was a detailed, exhaustive, humbling and grateful list.

Elijah's story had gone global. He refused to accept donations from corporations. He did not stay in any hotels during his three-month campaign. He had primarily hitch-hiked and couch-surfed across Canada. Every other mainstream politician in the world suddenly looked like an entitled, wealthy, taxpayer-abusing, pork-barrelling, trough-guzzling pig when compared to Elijah.

"Good evening. Well, this is the day that many Canadians have been waiting for. It's October twenty-first and polling stations across the country have been reporting record turnouts," Peter Bridgeman informed CBC viewers. "First, let me say that it has been my honour and privilege to cover elections with the CBC since 1972." The screen briefly showed the very dapper 1972 version of Bridgeman announcing election results from the fall of that year.

"In my opinion—and this opinion is shared by many from coast to coast—this past eleven weeks on the campaign trail has been the most exciting and controversial campaign in our nation's history. The campaign is now over. It is election night, and our CBC team will have in-depth coverage of the results from now until two a.m. Polls have just closed in our easternmost province. We take you now to Rex Mercer in Newfoundland and Labrador."

"Thank you, Peter. As our more experienced viewers may recall, I have often said that politics in Newfoundland and Labrador is a blood sport." CBC viewers were again transported through the "way back" machine, to a young Mercer reporting on provincial politics in 1973. "Newfoundlanders and Labradorians are notoriously feisty and ferocious regarding all matters politic," he continued wryly, with trademark raised brow. "Our gladiators have certainly not disappointed during this campaign."

The footage behind the commentator showed several clips which had gone viral recently. The first was a fist fight between two ladies—the Conservative candidate versus the IPP hopeful in Avalon—which had taken place during a televised debate. As popular as a girl fight might be to internet viewers, the "Fogo Island Fish Fight" was off the charts. The IPP candidate was up on charges for cold-cocking his Liberal adversary with a codfish. Earlier in the day, the Japanese media proclaimed the clip as the most-viewed YouTube video in Japanese Internet history. Ever.

"Peter, the first of our polling stations are reporting now. I will remind our viewers that these are early results. Siobahn O'Meara, the outspoken pugilistic IPP candidate is leading in Avalon, with three of eighty-nine polls counted. In the bellwether riding of St John's East, the heavily favoured Liberal incumbent, Nick Williams, is behind early to Jonny White of the IPP with five of one hundred and twenty-one polls reporting…"

There are six time zones in Canada spanning five-and-a-half hours. Bridgeman continued to quarterback the election results—smoothly switching to numerous correspondents, then back to HQ—as polling stations closed across Canada from east to west. Following early results from Newfoundland and Labrador, the Atlantic provinces—Nova Scotia, Prince Edward Island and New Brunswick—were the next to begin submitting results.

"Let's go now to Cardigan, Prince Edward Island, with Yvette Poirer…"

"Peter, as you know, this battle for Cardigan has been a dogfight between…"

"…With twenty-one of seventy-seven polls reporting, the IPP candidate in Acadie-Bathurst has a significant lead over…"

"…We are now declaring that the IPP has won three of Newfoundland and Labrador's seven seats, with four more races too close to call…"

"…Early results from Quebec are closer than polls indicated, as the Bloc Quebecois appears to be losing in many of their traditional strongholds. Remember, however, these are early results with only seven of one hundred and eleven polls reporting in…"

"…In 2015, Dustin Trudel's Liberal Party took all thirty-two seats in Atlantic Canada. It was the beginning of a landslide Liberal majority, that now appears in jeopardy four years later…"

The Mouse Who Poked an Elephant * 147

"…To Canada's largest city now, where Elijah has received 53 per cent of the popular vote in Toronto Centre…"

"…Twenty-two-year-old Juliette Sparks, the president of her student union at St. Mary's University has run a surprisingly well organized grassroots campaign in Halifax…"

"This is Jim Ingram from Canadian Forces Base Shilo Manitoba. Peter, with twenty-two of eighty-three polls counted, the Independent candidate Sergeant Suzanne Sullivan, a medic and victim of an IED attack in Kandahar, has a slight lead on the NDP incumbent…"

"Richard, is it safe to say that young voters—those under forty—are the biggest supporters of the Independent People's Party?"

"Peter, in Saskatchewan, that's a safe statement for sure. The IPP has certainly campaigned on a platform promising change. That appeals not only to the younger voters disaffected by traditional party politics, but also to the recently unemployed…"

"…Alberta, once considered an impregnable fortress for the federal and provincial Conservative Party, is having the closest races in recent memory…"

At 10:45 p.m. Eastern Standard Time, Peter Bridgeman shocked Canada, and the world with this statement: "It's the most controversial and unexpected election result in Canadian history. CBC News is now declaring that the Independent People's Party will form a majority government. Just hours ago many mainstream political analysts and the polls were predicting a Liberal minority.

"The IPP is elected or leading in one hundred and ninety-six ridings, the Liberals elected or leading in forty-nine ridings, the Conservative Party elected or leading in forty-six ridings, the New Democratic Party elected or leading in twenty-six ridings, the Green Party elected or leading in four ridings.

"We take you now to the Liberal Party headquarters in our nation's capital, where outgoing Prime Minister Dustin Trudel is scheduled to give a concession speech."

CHAPTER 10.
Canada Did What Now?

Most Canadians were hungover in some shape or form the morning following the election.

A lot of people who considered themselves among the "99 per cent" were hung over from partying and celebrating the IPP's unprecedented victory.

Most financially secure baby boomers were far sicker from dread, sadness, shock and despair. To be fair to the boomers who fit that description, if your life is good, not many of us want to embrace radical change. Even those people who neither drank nor used drugs were operating on less sleep, and/or messed up on some combination of hope, fear, jubilation or rage. The few Canadian newspapers still in business saw a brief spike in sales as people were buying the paper to archive the headlines from this momentous occasion.

"A BRAVE NEW CANADA?" asked the *New York Times*.

"IPP WINS SHOCKING MAJORITY!" trumpeted the *Globe and Mail*.

"CANADA'S NEW GOVERNMENT," pronounced the *Guardian*.

"A RADICAL RESULT," exclaimed the *Vancouver Sun*.

Around noon, Elijah started to get calls of congratulations from other world leaders.

Like Queen Elizabeth II. (She couldn't say so publicly of course, but she actually agreed with a few of Elijah's ideas.)

Elijah also took quick calls from the PM or president of India, Norway, Russia, Australia, South Africa, Brazil and about twenty more. Most calls were very quick and congratulatory in nature. Elijah was pleasant and concise during each call—at least, he was until he got a call from Washington.

"Elijah here."

"Yes. Hello. This is Washington. Vice President Pens would like to speak with the new Canadian prime minister."

"Hey, you sound surprised that I'm answering my own phone Anyhoo, you got him. Hello, Mr. Vice President. This is Elijah."

"Mr. Prime Minister—congratulations on your recent victory."

"Thank you, sir. The Donald made you call me, didn't he?"

"Ahhhhh…Mr. Prime Minister, the president of the United States is a very busy man, and…"

Elijah interrupted smoothly. "Mr. Pens—it's OK. You don't have to bullshit me. I really don't like your president, and I believe I have made that point very clear on numerous occasions. If he's busy, it's because he's tweeting about *SNL*'s latest skit which clearly highlights what a moron he is. So it's for the best that you called anyway, because I would not have taken your boss's call."

Now it was Mr. Pens turn to interrupt. "Now listen here, my young friend. This is a dangerous way to begin a relationship with your biggest trading partner."

"Mr. Vice President, we may share a border, but other than that you and I have nothing in common. Your current administration's greed, stupidity and lack of environmental stewardship is the single largest threat to global peace and safety the world has ever witnessed Therefore, it is highly unlikely that we will ever be friends. Please convey this message to your president."

Click.

President Trimp had been listening in to the call, but could not hold his silence any longer. "Why you insolent little piece of sh—"

The vice president sighed on the other line. "Save your breath, sir. He hung up on us."

Elijah addressed the Canadian public via television at 2100 hours Eastern Standard Time. He was wearing a gold Nehru jacket, white Aladdin pants and a green fez. He was sitting on a park bench with the Parliament Buildings in the background

"Hey, Canada. First, I need to thank everyone who voted in yesterday's election. It doesn't matter who you voted for—it just matters that you voted. So, thank you."

"Next, everybody just take a deep breath. Got it? Good. Now let it out and just breathe normally. There is no reason to panic. The Independent People's Party campaigned on change. And indeed, the IPP intends to change the way we run our country. We will do this because the majority of Canadians realize that change is necessary. Many of our current practices are economically or environmentally unsustainable, or put large corporations ahead of individuals."

Elijah paused to take a sip of water. "So I'm asking tonight for your understanding. I'm asking for you to try and see the positive benefits of the changes we will propose. In some cases the changes that we propose might make you afraid or feel threatened for the lifestyle that you have become accustomed to. If that is the case, it is likely that you are in a very comfortable place in life."

Elijah stood up, and the camera zoomed in closer. "So if you are very comfortable, and life has been good for you, all we are going to try and do is make some changes that will allow more people to have a more comfortable lifestyle." As he continued to speak, the camera cut away to a kaleidoscope of people across Canada.

Most of the people in the montage looked as if they had just auditioned for *Les Misérables*. "I 'm just asking that we see the future as a time to improve our country, and help each other."

The camera followed Elijah as he walked toward the Parliament Buildings and talked. "So, for now, be good to each other. Don't argue with people who have a different view than your own. I'll be meeting with the Governor General tomorrow, and we'll discuss forming government and a date for convening Parliament. We have a lot of good ideas to help out Canadians in need, and we are keen to get to work. Power to the people. Love peace and chicken grease.." The camera zoomed out, and showed Elijah stopping to throw a Frisbee with some people in the park.

In the days that followed the election Elijah and the new Independent members of Parliament moved very quickly on a number of issues.

Elijah selected twenty-seven Cabinet ministers two days after the election, and introduced them on television in his former time slot from his days hosting *Power to the People*. He surprised a lot of people by including five ministers who were not Independent members of Parliament.

Former prime minister Dustin Trudel, now the leader of the official opposition Liberal Party, accepted a position as minister of foreign affairs.

The minister of defence from the previous Liberal government, Harjit Singh, retained his Cabinet position.

The minister of employment and labour was from the New Democratic Party.

The minister for environment and climate change was the leader of the Green Party.

Minister for infrastructure was the former Conservative Party critic for that Cabinet position.

The remaining twenty-two people selected as Cabinet ministers from the IPP were not exactly household names.

Juliette Sparks— one of the youngest members of Parliament ever elected at twenty-two— became the youngest Cabinet minister in Canadian history as minister of youth.

Charley Shackleton was appointed minister of agriculture.

Danni GreyEyes—a former band chief of the Mistawasis First Nation was the new minister of Indigenous and Northern affairs.

Suzanne Sullivan—a recently retired medic from CFB Shilo was the new minister for status of women. (Canadian Forces members who win an elected position in public service must immediately release from the military.)

Dr. Andre Silverberg—a former federal prisoner who served four years for assisting incurable patients with medically assisted deaths—was appointed as minister of health.

Benjamin Big Canoe was the new minister for international trade.

Siobahn O'Meara from Avalon in Newfoundland was the new minister of fisheries and oceans.

Less Izmore—former elder of the Simpletons—was the new minister of finance.

Over the next few days the mainstream media had a field day reporting on these new Cabinet ministers:

"…Is taking our new fisheries minister to court on assault charges relating to an alleged assault during a debate…"

"Yes, I know he was a senior bank executive, but the new minister of finance hasn't worked in the commerce sector since 1988. Since then, he's been an elder in a commune that didn't use money in any way…"

"How a twenty-two-year-old can be expected to perform capably as a member of Parliament, let alone as a Cabinet minister, is beyond ridiculous."

"…None of these people have any political experience."

"Canadians threw the baby out with the bath water in this last election…"

Meanwhile, the Governor General approved that Parliament reconvene eight days after the election (a new land speed record for resuming Parliament, which eclipsed the old mark by twenty-two days).

The Canadian public was now alternately terrified or jubilant (depending on their political leanings) at the efficiency and effectiveness with which their new Parliament got down to business.

"Next, we take you to our Canadian correspondent in Ottawa, Eileen Murphy. Eileen, is the new Canadian government beginning to settle in?"

"Malcolm, new is certainly the best way to describe this government. None of the one hundred and ninety-six members of Parliament from the Independent People's Party have ever held an elected office at a federal level. Despite being political newcomers, and still trying to find their offices, they have hit the ground running. On the second day of Parliament, an Independent member's bill from Minister of Finance Less Izmore proposed that pay for members of Parliament and senators be reduced by 25 per cent effective immediately.

"The Bill further proposed a re-working of the pension plan for those two groups, essentially reducing future pension payouts to all MPs and senators by 60 per cent. As Independent members enjoy a majority in both the House of Commons and the Senate, the Bill is expected to pass easily and may come into effect as early as next week. Malcolm, passing a bill this quickly would be considered light speed for almost any country's political system.

"So in Canada, where the pace of parliamentary progress has previously been described as 'glacial' and 'ponderous,' this is truly remarkable."

"Eileen, how has this news been received by Canadian citizens?"

"Malcolm, I've been talking to people on the street from all walks of life, and haven't been able to find anyone who thinks it's a bad idea to pay politicians less money."

"Thanks for this, Eileen. Next we take you to Washington, where environmentalists are protesting President Trimp's decision to..."

Meanwhile, watching Parliament operate on CPAC—the Cable Public Affairs Channel—was the hottest new show on Canadian TV.

Speaker: The House recognizes the honourable minister for health.

Minister: Thank you, Madame Speaker. Regarding Independent Member's Bill C-447, the "Food Additive Tax." Colleagues, we have discussed this issue at some length. Well-informed Canadians understand and agree with the medical community that overly processed foods, and foods, drinks and snack items that are high in glucose, fructose, sugars, syrups, milled grains and saturated fats are responsible for the obesity epidemic our country currently faces. Obesity, and obesity-related medical issues, are the most significant contributor to rapidly rising medical costs for our public health care system. Bill C-447 proposes a food additive tax of 100 per cent. (*Jeering, angry shouts and catcalls from opposition MPs. The minister of health waits patiently for quiet.*)

"…A food additive tax of 100 per cent on the sale price on all those processed foods identified in Health Canada's list of overly processed foods." *As the minister continued to speak, the Health Canada list of foods that would be subject to the FAT tax roll across the bottom of TV screens on a banner:*

"SOFT DRINKS SWEETENED WITH SUGAR / ASPARTAME / SUCRALOSE / GLUCOSE / FRUCTOSE AND CONTAINING PHOSPHORIC ACID…"

Minister: Bill C-447 proposes that the food additive tax be implemented on 1 February, 2020, to allow manufacturers and merchandisers of these items time to slow production and adjust stock levels. The revenue from this tax will be used to subsidize Canadian farmers, fishermen and food distributors in the production and distribution of healthy and affordable food items—meats, fish and shellfish, vegetables and legumes, grains, fruits, and dairy items. Over time, the consumption of healthier fresh foods rather than processed foods filled with chemical compounds will inevitably result in healthier Canadians. (*The minister takes his seat to applause from Independent members.*)

Speaker: The House recognizes the honourable member from Charlottetown.

"TWINKIES, PIZZA POPS, RAMEN NOODLES…"

MP: Madame Speaker, as the Liberal critic for health, we strenuously object to this tax. A tax of this nature punishes the poorest people in Canada, and will do great damage to single parent families. Such families traditionally can only afford processed foods, as fresh non-processed foods have not been affordable for our poorest citizens. Beyond the cost factor, many families, and especially single parent families, do not have the time to prepare the traditional "cooked from scratch" family meals that seem to exist only in the minister's utopian society. In addition to this, the food processing industry employs some three hundred thousand people across Canada. This tax, if implemented, will result in massive layoffs for those workers. What does the minister of health propose those people do for a living? (*MP sits to applause from some Liberals.*)

"SNACK FOODS SUCH AS CHIPS, PRETZELS, CRACKERS, CHEEZIES..."

Speaker: "The House recognizes the honourable member from Cardigan."

MP: "Madame Speaker, honourable colleagues. The honourable member from Charlottetown understandably has some concern. After all, his family's business as Atlantic Canada's leading manufacturer and distributor of potato chips, snack foods and soft drinks may soon be less profitable." (*Cheers from Independents, angry boos from Liberals.*)

"However, as the minister of health alluded, revenue generated from the food additive tax will be used to subsidize the cost of growing and distributing healthy less processed foods. I will suggest that this revenue will create employment on Canadian farms and in the preserving and distribution of wholesome foods." (*Cheers from Independents, raspberries from Liberals.*)

ENERGY DRINKS SUCH AS: REDBULL, ROCKSTAR...

Speaker: "The House recognizes the honourable member from Mirabel."

MP: "*Madame, chers collègues.* À mon avis le nouveau tax..."

The Member's words were being translated from French to English on the banner across the bottom of the screen for viewers at home. (And for quite a few IPP members, who spoke no French.)

MP: "In my opinion, this new tax...oversteps the authority of elected officials.... A tax of this nature tells average Canadians...you aren't smart enough to make good decisions about what you should or should not eat... and therefore, we, your government will now control what you should or should not eat...this proposed new tax is an insult to Canadians...and indicates that our new government seeks to control Canadians' lives at one of the most personal levels.... We see this as a base attack on the freedom of Canadians to choose...the manner in which they live their lives." (*Some cheering from all sides of the House.*)

Speaker: "The House recognizes the honourable prime minister."

PM: "Look, let's be honest with each other. Most people understand that consuming too many processed foods like pop and Twinkies and chips is bad for us. The food additive tax is no different than the significant taxes we put on other unhealthy consumer items like cigarettes and alcoholic beverages. Our government has often stepped in and made laws to protect Canadians from making poor decisions. Seatbelts and motorcycle helmets? These things used to be optional. But they are now the law because they save lives."

Elijah made quotation marks with his fingers as he continued. "'Freedom' doesn't guarantee individuals the right to make stupid choices, and then expect society to fix things when stupid choices lead to poor results. Because after a lifetime of poor nutritional choices, individuals will become ill, and then they will look to our publically funded health care system to save them."

Elijah pressed on. "The purpose of this tax is not to make chips and pop and unhealthy processed foods illegal. If you want to eat an unhealthy diet, go ahead. But, if you make that choice, the tax revenue we collect on your purchase will help, in some part, to defray the growing cost of health care. The FAT tax is a very good way to discourage people from making poor choices all the time." Elijah grinned at the cameras in the House. "Consider the money you spend on the FAT tax as a down payment on your future health care needs.

"But there is more to it than that. As explained by our minister of health and by the minister of national revenue—the tax revenue raised by the FAT tax will be used to subsidize locally produced healthy foods. So that box of Pizza Pops that was five dollars is soon going cost you ten dollars if we can pass this bill. (*Jeers and catcalls from across the floor.*) Elijah waited, smiling, for the jeering to stop.

"But instead of Pizza Pops, you'll soon be able to be able to buy some real food—raised by local farmers and sold in local markets—fresh vegetables, fresh meats, fresh dairy, fresh fruits for reasonable prices. This is the purpose of the FAT tax. It's an investment in the future health of Canadians. It will, over time, reduce obesity-related illnesses among Canadians."

Elijah appealed now to the viewers at home through the CPAC cameras. "Look, if you work in a factory that makes sugar-coated whammy pops, and similar items that we intend to tax heavily, you are likely worried that this new tax will result in you being laid off. That is a valid concern. So, we are going to work in conjunction with Employment Canada on this issue. And if you lose your job as a result of the FAT tax, you will have first opportunity at the new jobs created in the local agricultural, food processing and food distribution sectors."

The new PM spoke as if he were in your kitchen or at a coffee shop. "Bottom line, Canada. The foods that make it on this list for the FAT tax are bad for your health if eaten regularly. They are cheap and affordable because they contain lots of sugars, flours, chemicals and toxins. Within a few months, you will be able to afford to buy real whole food again--and that's a win for all of us." Elijah took his seat to cheers and applause from the Independents. Not many of the members of Parliament across the floor jeered this time.

It was time to vote.

Later that afternoon, Lumpy, T-Bone and many other similar-minded entrepreneurs across Canada bought a staggering amount of canned pop, chips, energy drinks, Twinkies and Mr. Noodles.

"Dude, we are gonna make a killing on this after February first!" was the common sentiment of future FAT tax evaders from Twillingate to Tofino.

CHAPTER 11.

Unlikely Soldiers

"Lumpy."

"What?"

"Wake up, dude. We gotta be at the armoury in twenty minutes."

"Not gonna happen. I'm not joining the army. Especially not any army that tries to get me outta bed before noon."

"Well, this draft letter says if you don't show up for screening, you can be arrested, or your pogey cheque can be stopped, so…"

"Ain't gonna happen."

"All right, dude. Good luck. I'm gonna check it out."

T-Bone made it to the armoury just in time. There was a gaggle of people of various shapes and sizes near the walls by the amoury doors. There were some tables at the back of the room, where about fifteen militia members were talking quietly. At precisely eight o'clock, those military members came to attention and marched smartly toward the armoury doors. They halted, and did a turn to face the draftees. The smallest of them took two paces forward.

"Good morning. Welcome to the Hamilton Armoury. My name is Sgt. Lee. We have a lot to do today to get you started in the militia, so listen carefully to the instructions from our personnel in uniform. First, I want everyone here to line up with their toes on one of these three yellow lines." The sergeant was a slim Chinese-Canadian lady in her early thirties. The yellow lines she pointed to formed an open-sided square, about twenty metres on each side. She waited patiently.

For about seven seconds. People were sort of shuffling about listlessly and talking amongst themselves, so Sergeant Lee did what all drill sergeants do with new recruits. She snapped: emotionally, audibly, visibly.

"Stop moving. Look at me and listen carefully. Stop talking." Her voice had gone up an octave, risen by about forty decibels and taken on a "don't try me" tone. "These are simple instructions. You don't speak unless we ask you a direct question. And you sure don't need to shuffle about like brain dead zombies." She walked quickly toward two teenage boys who were giggling.

They stopped as the sergeant approached. "Do you find this funny?" Sergeant Lee asked the boys. She was about four centimetres in front of them, way inside what most people consider their comfort zone. They shook their heads.

"I can't hear you," Sgt. Lee persisted. "I asked you both a direct question. The question was, "Do you find this funny? Your possible answers include 'Yes, Sergeant' or 'No, Sergeant.'" It was quiet for a second.

"I still can't hear you!" Sgt. Lee shouted.

"N-no, Sergeant," both boys managed to stammer out.

"Then don't laugh." Sgt. Lee replied sweetly. She stepped back, wheeled about, and resumed her place in the centre of the armoury.

"So, as I was saying, in a moment you will get your toes on one of these three yellow lines. You will do it quickly, and you will do it without speaking. *Move NOW!*" Her voice cracked like a whip. *That's better*, she thought.

"All right. If any of you here for screening today are carrying any weapons, or any personal effect that may be considered a weapon—a pocket knife, fixed blade knife, fingernail scissors, brass knuckles, a pistol, pepper spray—put them in this bin now."

Sgt. Lee nudged a grey washtub on the floor with her foot. "If what you are carrying is not illegal, it will be returned to you at day's end. If what you are carrying is illegal, we will turn it in to the police as a surrendered item—your name will not be used." As several recruits came forward, the militia staff wrote names on the items with masking tape.

"Swiss Army knife- Bremner.

Pepper Spray- Ighedibo.

Water pistol? Landriault.

Box cutter-Smithson."

"Next," Sergeant Lee continued. "Cell phones?" Almost every hand went up.

Sgt. Lee gritted her teeth. "If you are raising your hand to ask me if you may keep your cellphone on your person, the answer is no. I am keenly aware that you are deeply attached to your phones, but you can watch cat videos and comment on Emily's new profile picture after you are dismissed." The hands went back down.

"Switch them off, and write your name legibly on the tape provided. Put the name tape on your phone. Hand your phone to one of these three corporals—they will record that you had a phone. It will be returned to you at the end of training today."

"Anybody else? No? Then we'll carry on. You first twenty people—" she pointed at them "—go with Cpl. Jones. Cpl. Jones led the group to the desks at the back of the room. "You next twenty, go with Cpl. Mascheretti.".

T-Bone and his new friends were screened—identity verified, fingerprints taken, military photo ID made.

He (barely) completed an aptitude test. "We'll debrief you this afternoon—the aptitude test is an indicator of which military occupations you are best suited for," the cute master corporal explained. "Questions?"

"So I could be a pilot?" T-Bone asked.

"Like I said, you'll be debriefed this afternoon."

"Fill out this medical questionnaire honestly," the medic was explaining. "It is a criminal offence to lie on any of these documents. What you are being offered here today is an opportunity—an opportunity to get some valuable training, and be paid for it. An opportunity to serve your country. If you make up a medical condition that you don't have in an effort to avoid this training, you will be caught, and you may be punished. Conversely, if you have a valid medical condition, don't try to hide it from us. We need to know so that we can train you safely."

Height- 172 cm
Weight- 85.4 kg

Resting pulse- 88

BP- 135 / 94

After the medical, they did a physical fitness test: shuttle run, push-ups and sit-ups. In his group of twenty, T-Bone came in eighth.

"All right, we are gonna take a twenty minute break for lunch. There are two washrooms behind me. I want everybody to go there now." As the group started to move, Cpl. Jones added, "Make sure you wash your hands before you come back out."

Lunch came in a small cardboard box. One apple. One ham sandwich on whole wheat, one bag of carrot and celery sticks. One bottle of water. One Wet-Nap. Full stop.

Cpl. Jones wandered among the recruits as they ate. They were seated at three tables. "Yes—you have a question?"

"Is there, like, a vegan option?" a girl asked timidly.

"Of course there is," Cpl. Jones replied. "Pass me your sandwich. Anybody wanna trade an apple and a bag of carrots for a ham sandwich?" Cpl. Jones asked the recruits.

T-Bone's hand was up in a flash.

"Here you go—now have your vegan option." Cpl. Jones handed T-Bone the sandwich, and gave the carrot sticks and apple to the girl.

"All right, listen up. Lunch is over. If there is anything you didn't unwrap or open, put it in this container—we'll reuse it for tomorrow's lunches. Next, unfold the boxes, and stack them neatly here. Now, open your Wet-Nap and wipe down the table where you were sitting. All done? Good. Come with me."

"Well, good afternoon. Once again, I am Master Corporal Negreira. As I promised this morning, we are going to debrief you on the results of your aptitude tests. Everyone was successful, and for the next few months of your training you will be trained for and employed as general military personnel.

T-Bone raised his hand, but the master corporal waved him off. "Currently, we don't need to identify any of you as 'gifted' or begin training anyone as a pilot or a sniper or anything other than general military."

T-Bone lowered his hand slowly. "Questions?" There were none. "Then go with Cpl. Jones, and good luck with your training."

"This is the quartermaster's storeroom. You are going to be issued some pieces of a uniform. You will be expected to wear this uniform whenever you are training and working with the militia. Once you have been issued your kit, go to that locker room and put on this uniform. You will be issued a padlock and there are two hundred empty lockers in there. Before we go in, fall in on that line, shoulder to shoulder. Everybody look up here."

Click, click.

"I always like to take a picture of our new recruits on Day One. If you are lucky, someday I'll tell you why. Now, go get your kit, change, lock up your personal belongings, and all your extra kit and get back out here."

Backpack - 1
Padlock- 1
Boots - Combat- 1 pair
Socks- Combat- 2 pairs
T-Shirt- Combat- 2

Pants- Combat - 2 pairs
Belt- Webbed- 1
Shirt - Combat- 2
Ballcap- Service (black)- 1

As the recruits trickled out of the locker room, Cpl. Jones made them name tags with masking tape and a black marker.

"Name?"

"T-Bone"

Cpl. Jones looked up and sighed. "Your family name is T-Bone?"

"Oh, sorry. Brown."

Cpl. Jones wrote "Brown" on the masking tape, cut it and handed it to Brown. "Put this on the strip above your right breast pocket. And fall in on that line with the rest of your new friends."

He turned and addressed the group. "If you are still with us after five training days, we'll order you some proper sewn on name tags." He moved in closer to the group, and his tone became softer, friendlier.

"Listen. What you are now wearing is a uniform—from the Latin meaning 'one form.' It makes all of us look similar. It identifies you as a member of the Canadian militia- to other militia members, to other organizations, and to civilians. All organizations have a set of standards—how we expect you will dress, and how you will comport yourselves, individually and in group settings. So, let's work on some of those standards."

Cpl. Jones stepped back one pace and snapped rigidly to attention. *And maybe flipped on a crazy robot switch?* Brown wondered.

"This is the position of Attention," Cpl. Jones shouted from his ramrod straight body.

"It is the first of many drill movements you will learn.

"Notice that the heels are together, and that there is a fifteen degree angle of separation between the big toes of each foot.

"Notice that the knees are locked firmly in place.

"Notice that the arms are held rigid and straight at the sides, fists closed, palms facing each leg, and that the thumb is in line with the seam of the trousers.

"The shoulders and shoulder blades are back.

"The stomach is in.

"The chest is out.

"The spine, the neck and the head are held high, level and erect, eyes looking straight ahead.

"From this point forward, you will be collectively known as Two Platoon. So when you hear me, or any other militia member shout 'Two Platoon,' you should anticipate that an order will follow."

"Two Platoon. AT-TEN-TION!" The odd collective of humans now known as Two Platoon may have tried their best to come to attention, but Cpl. Jones clearly wasn't happy, based on the volume and descriptive colour of his criticism.

After thirty minutes of drill, Two Platoon had a water break and then marched (not very well, according to Cpl. Jones) into a small theatre.

"Halt. Left turn. In single file, take a seat in those first two rows."

After a moment, One Platoon and then Three Platoon also filed in. Sgt. Lee crisply marched to a spot front and centre. She halted, then executed a smart turn to face the recruits. "Shut your pie holes!" she shouted at the few recruits foolish enough to be whispering in hushed tones.

The theatre went quiet. "We need you to watch a short film." Sgt. Lee explained sweetly and quietly. "It's going to help explain why you are here today. Do not speak or whisper during the film—it is disrespectful, and you will anger me."

Sgt. Lee marched off, and the film began. The Canadian prime minister appeared on the screen. And there was a small buzz in the room.

"Hello, recruits. Thanks for being at the Hamilton Armoury today. At this point, you should probably not be whispering to your new friends, because that will upset Sgt. Lee. A word of advice—please don't get Sgt. Lee upset. She will apparently rip your head off and, or, gouge your eyes out if you anger her. She and your other training staff members are just trying to complete your training in the most efficient manner.

"All right, I want to explain why we are drafting two million Canadians into the militia over the next twelve months. In accordance with the Militia Act we recently passed in Parliament, we see the militia as a way to gainfully employ Canadians on a part or full-time basis during a period of economic instability. From this point forward, all Canadian citizens under the age of twenty-five will be required to complete the ten-day basic militia training program that you are starting today. After completion of that training program, you will then be required to serve as a militia member for thirty days each year until you are sixty-five years of age. Here, meet some of your friends who have already joined our ranks."

The next two minutes were a veritable who's who of young Canadian pop culture icons and athletes and regular people—the clip showed them all working in uniform in the venues they described.

"Pte. Terry Milloy. Goalkeeper, Montreal Canadiens. I did landscaping this summer in Montreal parks."

"Pte. Trevor Wilson. I'm not famous. I was unemployed for the past eighteen months, now I'm planting trees in the Fraser Valley. The Militia Act has found me a full-time job."

"Ordinary Seaman Holly Bright. Part-time student, part-time health care worker.

"Pte. Justine Beaver. When I'm not recording, I'm training to work with autistic children."

"Pte. Juliette Sparks, Minister of Youth. When the House isn't in session, I'm a cook's assistant at a senior's complex."

"Pte. Quesnel Wei. I'm training as a medic. And studying to be a doctor, with funding through the Militia Act."

"Pte. Scarlett O'Brien. When I'm not rowing for Team Canada, I'm hoeing in this urban garden."

"Ordinary Seaman Lucas Cain. Quarterback, Toronto Argonauts. I'm training as a bosun with the Naval Reserve."

Elijah came back on the screen. "We need your help to make this work. We need your cooperation. I hope that you will see your time in the militia as an opportunity. An opportunity to receive a fair wage for a fair day's work. During your training, you'll be getting paid eighty dollars a day. Once you complete the basic militia training program, your pay will go up to one hundred dollars a day. You'll be assigned a job that best suits your skill sets and our needs. It could be park maintenance, picking up garbage, painting, cooking, snow-shovelling, minding seniors, working in a day care—the reason we drafted you at this time is because our records show that you have been unemployed for a while.

"Please don't be embarrassed by this fact. The unemployment rate is the highest it's been since the Great Depression in the 1930s. The only thing that ended the Depression then was World War Two.

"War is expensive, so we essentially spent our way out of the Depression building ships and planes and tanks and putting more than 11 per cent of our population in uniform to fight in World War Two. Right now there is no war, and we hope there never is again. But it is a crazy world out there, so it can't hurt us to be prepared in case we ever need to defend ourselves, or help another nation or ourselves during a natural disaster. So some of our newest members are volunteers, and that's all good. But the majority of our new members are being drafted.

"There are two ways that you can avoid having to serve in the militia if you receive a draft notice.

"You can pay the Receiver General for Canada $100,000.00, and $5,000.00 per year until you turn sixty-five.

"Or—two—you can go to jail for two years. This is a shitty option,'cause in our new prison system, we are gonna work the prisoners harder than militia members, and you don't get paid.

"So, we hope that you see this as an opportunity. You are gonna get some tremendous training. If you don't wanna carry a weapon ever or be trained on firearms, you can still serve. We can still use you.

"So, good luck with your training. Cooperate with your training cadre—these are good people.

"Don't act like dipshits, and they won't have to yell at you so much.

"It is my honour to serve as your prime minister. Love, peace and chicken grease."

Cpl. Jones flipped off the screen and brought up the house lights. Sgt. Lee was back out front.

"Questions?"

"Do you know Elijah? I mean, is he a friend of yours? Or...?" T-Bone asked.

"No, I don't know the prime minister. But he was smart enough to ask for our ideas to make the video better for all of us. We suggested adding the name of the staff sergeant at each armoury across Canada. So he did one hundred and fifteen takes of the line where he says 'Don't piss off Sgt. Blank, etcetera.'"

"Anybody else? Yes, Pte. Brown."

"When do we get to fire rifles and blow stuff up?" T-Bone asked.

"Weapons training will be given to those people who request it, usually after two months of training. We need to be certain we aren't giving a gun to an unstable person. Blowing stuff up? That isn't a skill set we need a lot of—we are building a nation here, not blowing stuff up."

After another fifteen or so minutes of questions regarding pay, travel, medical coverage, religious freedom, ethics and substance abuse, the room was quiet.

"All right. It's sixteen hundred hours. Be back here tomorrow morning at zero eight hundred hours. Be in your uniform—the same way you are dressed now. If you need to get personal items from your locker, you have five minutes. Delta Company, dismissed."

Lumpy was not in their apartment when T-Bone returned. T-Bone tried to call him, but Lumpy's phone was off. T-Bone cracked a beer, and scrambled some eggs. He fell asleep watching a hokey war movie.

"T-Bone- wake up."

"What the…what time is it? And where were you all night? And who are the guys by the door?"

"Uh, those two dudes are MPs. C'mon, if we hurry and get ready they're gonna give us a ride to the armoury."

"I thought you didn't wanna join the army," T-Bone shouted as he brushed his teeth.

"Yeah, well, I changed my mind," Lumpy replied. He didn't look well rested.

CHAPTER 12.
Pioneering

KT Burfitt absolutely loved SimpleTown. She had been there for more than a year, and had been unofficially adopted by Susanna. More Simpletons were moving to SimpleTown every day, and they needed to expand their territory. The town was a constant beehive of activity. Logs were felled to build new dorms, the subsequent cleared land was used for gardens and pastures, the meeting hall was expanded, a new waterwheel in the river powered a mill that ground flour and milled lumber…

Less Izzmore, Charley Shackleton and Elijah had visited SimpleTown briefly a month previous. It was a truly emotional reunion between Less and the Simpletons. Many of the older Simpletons were unaware that there had been an election, or that the prime minister—a former TV celebrity—was in their town. More recent arrivals knew who Elijah was, but he wasn't swarmed by groupies like almost everywhere else he went. He appreciated the fact that the SimpleTown visit was the most relaxing time he had spent in several years.

As an older farmer and a huge champion of environmental practices, Charley was brought to tears by how thoughtfully the Simpletons were protecting the land.

Elijah was amazed at the spirit of community, the spirit of cooperation, how good the food was, and how ridonculously banging the weed was. Less and Elijah even got Charley to try some.

"Well, this is way better than whisky and water," was Charley's famous quote, between giggle fits. "I don't know why I waited seventy-two years to try this."

During a big town hall meeting, Less, Elijah and Charley explained to the Simpetons that SimpleTown was gaining worldwide notoriety as a model community from a sustainability and cooperative perspective. They had several proposals for the Simpletons.

First: to set up SimpleTown as an international school of sustainability to accept ten co-op students/teachers a year from other international farms. The hope here was that best practices from other farms and countries could be trialled and practised here, and conversely, back at SimpleTowns in other countries and communities. After some discussion, this was approved.

Second: have willing Simpletons apply for pioneer land grants so that the land SimpleTown currently occupied (and literally thousands of acres around it) could be legally deeded in perpetuity to individuals and their heirs. This proposal was met with significant resistance, as many Simpletons believed that no human could own land; rather, they believed that humans were merely the caretakers of the land.

"Look, I agree with you in principle," Less said, "but in the interest of protecting this land for yourselves and all future Simpletons, it's best that we have some legal documentation in place. Please consider it as a small concession to satisfy some bureaucratic BS to safeguard the land for future generations. I can think of no better guardians of this beautiful way of life than you thoughtful and caring people."

Eventually the Simpletons agreed that SimpleTown as a collective community would make the application, and that five thousand acres would be deeded to them in accordance with the *Pioneer Act*.

Third: Elijah and Charley then explained the need for the sort of knowledge that the Simpletons had acquired. "Essentially, we need missionary farmers to spread the good word of Simpleton sustainability across Canada," was how Charley put it.

"We have a lot of new pioneers out there who are eager to work and learn but they are making some mistakes because they have no farming or homesteading experience," Elijah stated.

"Like planting potatoes in August," Charley interjected, "or cutting trees too close to riverbeds, and not knowing about composting, lambing, animal husbandry, contour ploughing…"

"So you are asking some of us to be volunteer teachers away from SimpleTown?" KT asked.

"Yes. There is a need for your skill sets on pioneer farms all across Canada. Think of it as being a Jesuit or a missionary who teaches sustainable farming and living."

The crowd was silent.

"Just think about it," Charley said. "We don't need an answer right away."

At a dance that night, Less introduced Charley to Dorothy. It turned out that they had both been big square dancers back in the day. It was love at first sight. A week later she volunteered to help a young couple at a pioneer farm near Charley's place in Elgin County. A week after that, Elijah married them at a civil ceremony on Charley's farm. The barn dance that followed was talked about for years after.

A month after Less, Elijah and Charley's visit, KT learned that her mom had been diagnosed with cancer. Her parents had separated years before, and her father was remarried, so he was sorry, but not sorry enough or in a position to be able to help his ex-wife.

KT and Susanna visited her mom, Jill, in a Vancouver hospital, and learned that she needed chemotherapy. In speaking to the doctor, KT learned that her mom would need homecare after each treatment. The doctor estimated the process might take three to four months. While taking her mom back to her house on the outskirts of Maple Ridge, KT noticed a help wanted poster attached to a pioneer farm sign.

"Mom, are you gonna be okay in the car for five minutes?" KT asked. "I just wanna talk to these people very quickly."

"I'll be fine, KT—I have Susanna here to keep me company." The two were quickly becoming good friends.

KT was back in two minutes. "It's perfect," she told Susanna and her mother.

"What's perfect?" Susanna and Jill asked simultaneously.

"I'll explain while we drive."

The next few days were busy for everybody. KT and Susanna returned briefly to SimpleTown to explain what was going on. KT was sad to be leaving SimpleTown, even for a short period of time, but Susanna was—understandably–very emotional. She had been raised by the people in this village. Many of the Simpletons believed that she had blacked out whatever horrible memories she might have had of her life before SimpleTown.

"Susanna, do you want to stay here in SimpleTown?"

"Yes." Susanna sniffled through some tears. "But I know you have to leave to help your momma, so I'll go with you." They each packed a few simple personal possessions, and after a heart-wrenching farewell from the Simpletons, they returned to KT's childhood home outside Maple Ridge.

"KT, you know you don't have to do this," her mother was saying. "You and this beautiful child have your own lives to live."

"Gramma, it's okay. We can go back to SimpleTown when you get better." KT and her mother both burst into tears.

Susanna rolled her eyes, and flipped on "Mr. TV."

"Yay! *SpongeBob Squarepants*," she said, sitting cross-legged about two feet in front of the screen, hypnotized.

She hasn't forgotten everything from her past, KT thought.

The Mouse Who Poked an Elephant ⋆ 183

KT alternated between days on the farm and driving her mother for treatment. Work on the nearby pioneer farm went well over the next few weeks. It had been a farm up until 1998, but had eventually gone into receivership as Canadians began to grow less of their own food and buy cheaper food imported from other countries. The land had begun to grow saplings, but it wasn't difficult to clear.

The new pioneers were Syrian refugees. Marwan Mahmoud had been a professor of mathematics at the university in Aleppo a few years ago. His wife, Reem, had been educated at the University of Damascus. They met at their wedding, which had been arranged by Marwan's and Reem's fathers. A week after the wedding, the university was unrecognizable. Whether the shells came from ISIS or government guns seemed of little consequence now.

The Mahmouds had twin boys: Ammar and Yaman. They were a year younger than Susanna, but it was clear that the boys were Susanna's project, and she kept them hopping from sun up to sundown. The three kids planted a two-acre garden on the first piece of cleared land.

Potatoes, corn, lettuces, peas, beans, zucchini, peppers, tomatoes, cucumber, cauliflower, squash, etc.

"Susanna, how do you get those boys to work so hard?" KT asked on the drive back to Maple Ridge.

"Fear is a great motivator," Susanna replied, putting on a mean face and brandishing a fist.

KT was too shocked to speak for a few seconds. "Who taught you to say that?"

"I can't remember."

"You haven't been hitting them? Have you?"

"Nope. But if they think I might hit them, then…"

"Susanna!" KT was horrified, wondering again what sort of monsters had raised Susanna before the Simpletons found her.

KT tried to get more info out of Susanna but the young girl was shutting down.

"I don't wanna talk anymore," she said, and then turned from KT. And despite KT's best efforts, the young girl remained silent on any topic regarding her past life.

While the kids planted the garden, KT arranged a deal with a nearby lumber mill. She traded cutting privileges on a four-acre woodlot for enough peeled logs to build the Mahmouds a home. They had been renting a nearby trailer, but couldn't afford to keep renting. The owner of the mill was impressed enough with the Mahmouds' "Pioneer Spirit" that he helped them build it.

The Pioneer Project was working well.

CHAPTER 13.
A Changing Nation

Ottawa

Dustin Trudel and Benjamin Big Canoe had just returned from Washington when they ran into Elijah in the rotunda. "Hey, just the two cats I needed to see. C'mon, take five and keep me current."

Elijah held the door to his office open. The three took a seat.

Dustin Trudel spoke first. "As we anticipated, the Trimp administration is not amused that we are backing out of NAFTA and CUFTA without waiting for their blessing. Although it's no secret that President Trimp wanted out of NAFTA, he wanted out on his terms. Essentially, he wanted to keep those parts of our trade agreements that were most favourable to the US, and discard the rest."

"And did you meet with The Donald personally, or…?" Elijah asked, smiling.

"No, the president was in the other presidential palace in Manhattan, with Mr. Sputin if the rumours are true. I spoke with Vice President Pens—"

"How is the vice president holding up these days?" Elijah interjected.

"He looked very tired."

"Poor bastard." Elijah did seem genuinely sorry for the vice president. "Trimp has delegated his whole job to Pens. Well, the whole job, except angry tweets. That is a sacred duty that only the POTUS can perform."

Trudel chuckled. Elijah's dislike for President Trimp was very common knowledge. Trimp felt the same way about Elijah; in fact, rumours abounded that he was trying to have Elijah assassinated by shadowy men from shadowy places. Some said it would be the CIA, others the FBI, a few more suggested the KKK…

For his part, Elijah utilized an alarming lack of security personnel: he had reassigned most of the PM's security detail to the militia training cadre, and often travelled with just a few trusted friends. Elijah was routinely asked by concerned citizens or the press if he was aware of the rumours regarding Trimp's plans to assassinate him.

Here was his famous answer to that question during an MTV interview:

"That would be awesome. What an honour. I mean, there is nothing better than a martyr to get people passionate about a cause. And if I got to pick the method of my death, I'd like to be crucified. No disrespect to Jesus, but a crucifixion can really get the crowd on your side. I know it would really suck on a personal 'I don't like pain' level, but think of the symbolism going forward. Anyway,

I'm just being silly. If President Trimp has me killed, there are plenty of smart and capable folks who could lead our nation."

"Any other news from Washington, Dustin?"

"Umm, I had an interesting meeting with the Oobimas."

"What are they up to?"

"They are fed up, and don't want to live in the States during Trimp's reign, so they applied last week to immigrate to Canada." Dustin Trudel was interrupted by hoots, hollers and applause from Benjamin and Elijah.

"They are actually at our place in Montreal now with Sophia and the kids. Michelle has been under a lot of pressure to run for the Democrats, but I don't think she's interested. Barack did ask a favour though."

"To fast track the application?" Elijah interjected.

"No, sir—the exact opposite. His favour is he doesn't want any favours—he doesn't want to be given priority treatment over anyone else."

"That's very smart. Is the American press aware of their intent to leave the US?"

"No. He's leaking it this afternoon. He's hopeful that this will be seen as the highest condemnation of Trimp's Administration, and lead to further calls for impeachment of the president."

Elijah was clearly delighted with this move by the Oobimas. "Well, it's a very courageous move on their part. I know they will take a lot of heat for this—they'll be called traitors, deserters…"

"They are a pretty tough family, Elijah. Oh, they'd love to meet you by the way. My place in Montreal this weekend?"

"It would be my honour. You pick the time and day—we'll do it." Benjamin grabbed Elijah's elbow and whispered in his ear as Elijah leaned closer. Elijah blushed a bit. "Umm, Dustin, I meant to say, ask Moneypenny when I'm free."

The Cabinet laughed. Elijah didn't like having staffers, until he double and triple-booked himself and missed scheduled appointments by not keeping a calendar. His Cabinet had convinced him that he needed a handler. Moneypenny's real name was Violet Harris. She was a retired schoolteacher who had taught Elijah to read and write when he arrived in Canada.

"Benjamin, same questions. What news from your meeting with the secretary of commerce?"

"Uhhh, it was pretty bad. He cancelled the meeting, and the US media did a one-sided story on the piece." Benjamin withdrew the *Washington Post* and read:

"The secretary of commerce believes that the Canadian economy and its people will suffer tremendously from their government's impetuous and illegal withdrawal from these longstanding trade agreements. The Government of the United States intends to take this matter to the highest international courts, where we will seek and inevitably receive *trillions* of dollars in damages for this illegal, irrational and ill-advised exit from existing trade agreements, etcetera, etcetera."

"Assholes. Did we find anyone willing to cover the other side of the story?"

"Umm, Meagan Kelly from NBC stepped up and had the secretary and I discuss the matter on television. Look. Listen." Benjamin handed Elijah his phone.

"With me today is the Canadian minister of trade, Benjamin Big Canoe, and the US secretary of commerce, Ross Wilbur. Minister, what are your thoughts regarding the secretary's comments with respect to the US taking Canada to court for breaking trade agreements?"

"Hi, Mr. Secretary, and hello viewers. Meagan, we aren't too worried about the United States taking Canada to international court in The Hague."

"You really should be worried," interjected the secretary of commerce.

Cut back to split screen that shows the secretary on the left and the minister on the right.

"Mr. Secretary, I believe I have the floor. Meagan, to be honest, we expected that this would be the default reaction from the US. Look, there is thirty years of indisputable empirical evidence that demonstrates anyone who does anything Donald Trimp dislikes gets threatened with court action."

"How dare you speak of our president—"

Meagan Kelly interceded now as moderator. "Mr. Secretary, I'll give you a fair chance to respond in one moment. Minister Big Canoe, please…finish your statement."

"Meagan, here is why Canadians shouldn't worry about this court case. The Hague has an enormous backlog of trade agreement cases dating back some fifteen years that are still waiting to be heard. In seventeen of these cases, Canada is actually seeking damages from the United States for a multitude of transgressions to NAFTA and CUFTA agreements on everything from auto parts to softwood lumber to crude oil. President Trimp was already in violation of NAFTA and CUFTA agreements. So NAFTA and CUFTA already weren't working.

"Also, viewers on both sides of the border should recall that President Trimp campaigned on a platform of ending these sorts of free trade agreements. The Trimp administration is just upset that we beat them to the punch. Regarding the international courts, the recent events with the abrupt and messy dissolution of the European Economic Community, and all of its associated trade agreements will back up the courts even further. This case won't be heard for at least thirty years, if it is ever heard at all."

"Secretary Wilbur, your response?" *Cut from split screen, close-up of secretary.*

"Well, I believe your minister of trade and your current Canadian government is badly underestimating the priority which will be placed on this particular suit for damages against Canada. The Canadian people should be aware Canada has historically enjoyed a significant trade surplus with the United States. More than 70 per cent of Canada's Gross Domestic Product each year since 1984 has been generated by trade." The secretary removed his glasses to continue.

"In layman's terms, the North American Free Trade Agreement and the Canada-US Free Trade Agreement were of tremendous value to the Canadian economy. Our department of commerce tried to negotiate openly and transparently with your current government regarding NAFTA and CUFTA amendments. Sadly, your government was unwilling to negotiate in any sense of the word. Therefore, as stated, the US has no alternative but to sue

Canada for damages through the international courts." *Back to split screen.*

"Secretary Wilbur has a good point," Benjamin agreed amiably. "NAFTA and CUFTA did increase cross border trade with the USA tremendously. But it's important to understand who made all that money." *Cut to close up of minister.* "You see, the increased revenue from these free trade agreements didn't make average individual Canadians richer, it just made big corporations richer. Free trade made a small percentage of rich people very much richer, and lowered the standard of living for almost everyone else—Canadians and Americans—who didn't own a big multi-national corporation. I do have a question for the secretary of commerce, though." *Close-up of minister looking serious.*

"Go ahead, Minister," urged Kelly.

"Yeah, uhhh, you're like a gazillionaire, right? So how many zeros are even in a trillion? I mean is a trillion bigger than a billion or a gazillion, or…?"

Cut back to Meagan. "The entire debate can be seen at www.cnn. As our viewers might imagine, the remainder of the dialogue between the minister of trade and the commerce secretary was very emotional and adversarial."

"Ooooo, nice one." Elijah was off and running. "Thanks guys, love ya. Dustin—racquetball at five, yes?" Elijah hustled out the door.

"Has he always been this…uhhh…" Dustin wasn't sure how to put it.

"Hyper? Informal? Irreverent? Yes."

Lac Champlain, Quebec

Telecorp of Quebec was set for the third take of the commercial shoot.

"And three, two, one, action."

"A MESSAGE FROM THE GOVERNMENT OF CANADA..."

Scene: a field, horses and plough in background.

"Hey, folks—I'm Charley Shackleton, your minister of agriculture."

"And I'm Raj Binder, your minister of citizenship and immigration."

Raj: "Recent global events have resulted in a humanitarian crisis. There are currently more than four hundred million refugees worldwide. These people are homeless, and many are starving."

Charley: "Canada has the lowest population density on the planet. So we are in a position to help our brothers and sisters."

Raj: "Effective July first, our nation's birthday, Canada will begin to increase immigration, with a goal of accepting one million new Canadians under the age of thirty each year."

Charlie: "Also effective on July first, Canada will launch our Pioneer Project. We have identified more than six hundred thousand plots of land to be made available to willing pioneers. These plots of land vary in size, from two acres up to one hundred acres. Appropriate tools and funds will be made available to successful applicants."

Raj: "The ideal Pioneer Project applicant also has an option to sponsor new Canadians, either in their existing homes or on new homesteads. Reimbursement for sponsoring new Canadians will be determined based on local cost of living indexes."

Charley: "Pioneer Project applicants must work on and improve the land they are given from an agricultural perspective. Those pioneers who meet the improvement criteria for five calendar years will be given their land. Listen, nothing in life is free—but if you are willing to put in some hard work, the Pioneer Project can help you create a legacy. Sounds a like a great deal, don't it, Fred?"

Fred: "Woof!"

Raj: "For more information on the Pioneer Project, and on sponsoring new Canadians, please visit www.gc/ca/pioneerproject."

"That's a wrap, people. Great job, gentlemen. You too, Fred."

Ottawa

Juliette Sparks was a workhorse. It was past ten p.m., but she was still crawling through a pile of correspondence. This one was a handwritten letter. *Who still does that?* she wondered.

The writing inside was a little spidery, but very legible.

To the Minister of Youth: The Honourable Juliette Sparks

4 August 2020

Dear Ms Sparks:

We had the privilege of meeting you in Moosejaw during the launch of the HomeShare program. My name is Rose Bishop, and I am 79 years old. My friend is Kate MacAloon and she is 83.

We have been staying with Trevor and Sherry Cluett and their 2 children in Moosejaw for the past three months. When we met, you asked us to keep you posted on how HomeShare is working for us, so here goes.

The HomeShare Program has been a blessing for all of us. Trevor and Sherry are hard-working people, but it's a tough economy out there. They have told us that the only way they could keep their house was to take in boarders to help with the cost of the mortgage, heat, lights, etc.

So, through HomeShare, Kate and I have each been paying the Cluetts $600.00 a month for a room which we share. They have 2 wonderful young children, whom Kate and I have been looking after. Sherry says this saves them another $1200.00 a month in childcare. Merciful heavens, things are expensive these days! Kate insists that I tell you we are also both very good cooks, and we keep a very clean house. She can't write much anymore 'cause her hands are stiff, but my goodness, that girl could talk the legs off a cast iron stove.

Kate lost her husband last year, and she wasn't happy (and couldn't afford to stay) in the Seniors' residence in Moosejaw. I was about to lose my tiny apartment in Moosejaw, as well, so Homeshare couldn't have come at a better time for us. I didn't want to spend my last years without a purpose. Now both Kate and I feel like we are helping somebody—the Cluetts—and they feel like they are helping us.

Sherry says to tell you that the kids call us Gramma Rose and Gramma Kate. They are adorable little children. Anyway, I know you are busy, so I'll sign off by saying this HomeShare program is a wonderful thing that is helping all of us. Thank you for having the common sense to see a solution in the problem of affordable housing for seniors and people who don't have a home.

Your friend, Rose Bishop

PS. Kate and Sherry say they think you and our young prime minister are an item? Haha.

PPS. Two days later. Kate didn't wake up this morning. The ambulance people who came were very nice, and they said Kate passed peacefully in her sleep. We are all very sad, but none of us live forever. Kate would have wanted me to tell you that she had a good run, and that your thoughtfulness ensured her last days were spent happily, with dignity and purpose.

Rose

"For our next story, we follow Rex Mercer as he investigates how the Simpleton policy is affecting Canadians, and gathering world-wide attention."

Cut to Rex.

"Thank you, Peter. This was a fascinating story to cover. Essentially the Simpleton policy gives tax breaks for work done by people or work done in the simplest methods, and applies an extra tax to products or goods that are made using robotics or complicated technology."

Cut to Rex in a dory with two fishermen.

"This is Dick and Jimmy Ryan from Joe Batt's Arm in Newfoundland. These men and their families before them had been fishing these waters for more than two hundred years, until overfishing and the moratorium on cod brought that way of life to an end."

Dick hauls in a fish, hand over hand.

"Jimmy, can you explain how this new Simpleton policy has helped your family?"

"Yes, B'ye, it's after puttin' some people back to work on a small scale. So I has an inshore licence that lets me catch fifty kilos of groundfish every day. And because Dick and I does the fishin' without fancy boats and sonar and radar and such, we get subsidized a dollar per kilo for the fish we sells. So later today, we can sell this fish for a cheaper price than what is catched up on the big factory freezer trawlers."

"And the fish from them bigger trawlers has a dollar per kilo tax on to it," Dick Ryan added. "Those big trawlers does a lot of damage- They takes too many fish and breaks up the ocean floor with heavy gear. The old people seen that coming back in the sixties when boats and the gear was g'tting' bigger and bigger." Dick hauled up his line and pointed to his gear. "Look here, Mr. Mercer—the same gear your grandfather's grandfather fished with. One jig and one man. Fishing by hook and line gives the fish a chance—some will always live to breed more fish. Young people today calls it sustainability—sure, that's fine— 'twas always just called common sense when Jimmy and I was pups."

"And the fish you are catching, where will it be sold?" Rex asked.

"Well, some we'll sell fresh, still twitchin', to local people who wants a nice feed o fish. We'll dry and salt the rest in our local cooperative—there's a tremendous hunger yet for salt cod in the Caribbean, and Spain and so forth." Jimmy handed his line to Rex.

"Here, haul this in, Mr. Mercer."

Camera fades back to show Rex, Jimmy and Dick in a dory. Close-up of a panting Rex hauling in a nice-size codfish.

"We sent Rex a little farther west for our next story," Bridgeman explained.

"This is Rex Mercer in St. Lambert, Quebec, at the Shellington Mill."

Camera shows waterwheel turning in background.

"This is Maureen Shellington, the great-granddaughter of the man who built this mill in 1904. Maureen, I understand the mill closed in 1972. Can you tell us how you were able to re-open?"

"Yes, with pleasure. First, we need people to understand that this mill employed eighty-five people from 1904 until we closed. We made top-quality tables and chairs from local sugar maple, but by the 1970s automation, cheaper materials and cheaper foreign labour priced our product out of the market."

Camera moving with Rex and Maureen walking inside the mill.

"So, all of this beautiful equipment sat idle for almost fifty years. Recently, we applied for a start-up grant under the umbrella of the Simpleton policy. We started with twenty people, but we intend to be back at eighty-five full-time workers shortly."

Camera switches to show a man and woman turning chair legs on a lathe.

"We have a contract to build four thousand school desks and chairs, plus a lot of private orders for our dining room furniture. Our pricing is competitive again because the Simpleton policy rewards us for using hand tools, water power and people power to build our furniture."

"And the import tax now being charged on furniture made outside Canada—has that helped your business?"

"Certainly. We couldn't compete without it."

Camera fades to show waterwheel turning.

"Rex is on the move again," the affable host exclaimed.

"This is Rex Mercer in Gimli Manitoba. I'm with Magnus Johannson, who is building straw bale houses. Magnus, we understand demand for bale houses is growing quickly?"

"Yes, we are very busy. You see, a bale house is eligible for a $20,000 rebate under the Simpleton Policy. It is a good way to build in Canada—the house is R 60—so it's easy to heat in the winter and to keep cool in the summer. We use barley straw from the local farmers, and stack the bales like bricks. Then we cover the straw with a stucco mix made from local clay, so all of our materials are available locally. It's an environmentally friendly way to build. And it's fun. Here, put on these rubber gloves. I'll show you what I mean."

Camera shows Rex and Magnus spreading stucco on the outside walls.

"From Gimli, Manitoba, this is Rex Mercer."

Cut back to studio, Peter and Rex.

"So, quite a road trip for you, Rex. In your opinion, is the Simpleton policy helping put Canadians back to work?"

"Yes, absolutely. The Simpleton policy essentially subsidizes any work that is done by hand—the less technology is involved in a process, the higher the subsidy. Conversely, those companies using more automation are penalized with a tax. But the Simpleton policy is also being applied in conjunction with two other pieces of recent legislation that are encouraging Canadians to buy locally-made goods. Bigger automated companies are paying a higher carbon tax for the power their plants would require, and for the fuel used in shipping their product. And finally, the import tax imposed on goods made outside Canada has ensured that goods made in Canada are priced as low, or lower than imported goods."

"Peter, three months ago the unemployment rate in Canada was at 15 per cent—today it's at 13 per cent and falling. Our government seems optimistic that these three new policies will continue to kick-start the Canadian economy."

"Finally, what do you make of President Trimp's threat to retaliate against these pieces of legislation? Specifically our withdrawal from NAFTA and the imposition of tariffs on imported goods?"

"Peter, there is a large and growing list of individuals, corporations and nations that President Trimp is upset with. But I suspect that the Canadian prime minister and our current government is at the top of that list."

"Any speculation on what sort of retaliation President Trimp may take?"

Close-up of Rex, looking thoughtful, eyebrow up.

"I believe it would be almost impossible to speculate on future events involving either the president or our prime minister. They are the two most unpredictable people we have ever seen in public office. Rather than attempt to divine the future—and almost certainly be wrong—I believe I would prefer to report on events after they have happened.

"Therefore, regarding my future as a fortune teller, I will leave you with this nugget. 'I prefer to remain silent and be thought a fool, as opposed to speaking out and removing all doubt.'"

Bridgeman smiled wryly as the director gave him the wrap-up signal. "Tune in tomorrow night for part two of our parliamentary progress report. I'm Peter Bridgeman. From all of our crew at CBC, thank you for watching, and good night."

CHAPTER 14.
A Cold Dark Winter

KT's mother had initially responded well to the treatment, and her initial cancer was in remission. Then the doctors discovered that her cancer had spread to her liver and stomach.

Between KT, Reem and Jill, they had been homeschooling Susanna and the twins as best they could. KT had broken down and got a cell phone again so that her mom could reach her on the farm. The salesgirl gave her a two-for-one deal, so KT bought her mom a phone, put her mom on the same plan, and disconnected their landline.

"We can try to treat this with chemotherapy again, but as you know, Mrs. Burfitt, the treatment will make you feel sick and tired." The young doctor paused for a minute, then added an afterthought. And of course, there's no guarantee that the chemotherapy will halt the cancer."

"Doctor, I am sick and tired of feeling sick and tired," Jill Burfitt replied. "Can I think it over? I want to discuss it with my daughter."

"You take all the time you need, but, if you decide to proceed with the treatment, the sooner we begin, the better our chances of success."

"I'll give you my decision by Monday morning," Mrs. Burfitt promised.

KT and Jill picked up Susanna from the Mahmoud farm on the way from the hospital back to Maple Ridge. It was a pretty quiet ride. KT had to pull over a few times to let Jill be sick.

Once they got home, KT went out to pick up some groceries.

Susanna fired up her new friend, Mr. Television.

A nice pot of tea, that's what I need, Jill thought.

"Okay, Mom, I'll be back in a few minutes. Love you." KT gave her mom a peck on the cheek and flew out the door.

Moments after KT left, Jill's phone rang.

"Hello?"

"Yes, may I speak with Jill Burfitt please?"

"May I ask who's calling?

"This is Sgt. Lena Adams from the RCMP detachment in Maple Ridge." The crisp and professional female voice continued. "Mrs. Burfitt, we need to act quickly. The RCMP have reason to believe that your daughter and the young girl in her care known as Susanna are in danger."

"Good heavens, what sort of danger?"

"Mrs. Burfitt, we have reason to believe that Susanna's parents might be looking for her."

Jill Burfitt was freaking out. She only knew a bit of Susanna's story, but it was enough to know that whoever could hurt a child like that was a monster. The sergeant was talking again.

"Mrs. Burfitt, I need you to remain calm and follow my instructions. Is Susanna with you?"

"Yes, she's here with me, but..."

"And where is your daughter?"

Jill was hyperventilating. "My daughter just went out for groceries. She will likely be home in twenty minutes or so, but..."

"Mrs. Burfitt, like I said, please remain calm. If you follow my instructions, we can keep everybody safe. Please confirm your civic address for us."

"It's 1611 Petunia Court."

"Thank you, Mrs Burfitt. Please stay on the line." There was a brief pause.

"Mrs. Burfitt, we'll have an unmarked car at your house in about two minutes. I need you to ensure that your front door is open."

"Okay, I just unlocked the front door."

"Good. Now, is your bedroom upstairs?"

"Well, yes, but what in the name of—"

"Mrs. Burfitt, we need you and Susanna to go upstairs to your room, and put yourself in the bedroom closet."

Jill was panicking, but she figured the RCMP must know what they were doing.

"Susanna, can you help me get upstairs, honey?"

"Sure, Gramma." Susanna clicked off the TV and started to race up the stairs. She stopped halfway up, came back down and helped Jill climb the stairs. "Gramma, are you talking to someone on the phone?"

"Yes, honey, it's just an old friend." Jill panted as they took the last two steps. *I don't want to scare the child—what do I tell her now?*

"Susanna, we are gonna play a little game. This friend of mine used to play hide and seek with me, and she's coming over now to play. So we are gonna hide in the closet and, in a minute, we'll hear her starting to look for us."

"Okay, cool!"

"Mrs. Burfitt, are you still on the line?" Sgt. Adams was asking.

"Yes, Sergeant. Susanna and I are in the closet. But what in the name of—"

"The next thing you hear will be an RCMP car pulling up in your driveway. Can you hear it?"

"Yes, they just got out of the car." From inside the closet, they could hear the car shutting off, and two car doors closing. Jill was trying to stay calm for Susanna, but she was having trouble catching her breath.

"Okay, our officers are going to enter your house, and make sure everything is clear, then they'll come upstairs to speak with you. You are doing great. Just stay calm, okay?"

Jill and Susanna could hear the officers down below. They closed the front door, went through the kitchen and living room…

Susanna shivered with anticipation as the footsteps climbed the stairs. She didn't understand why people needed phones to play hide and seek, but whatever.

"And here we are!" shouted the voice of Sgt. Adams.

A very dirty man had just flung open the door. Jill was confused. Sgt. Adams and the man with her looked like dirty, skinny crackheads from a movie set, not RCMP officers.

Susanna screamed louder than anything Jill had ever heard, until the man slapped her, slammed her hard against the closet wall and put a very dirty hand over her mouth. He held a knife up very close to Susanna's eye. "Hi, Susanna. Mommy and Daddy missed you, baby girl."

Susanna looked catatonic. Her body had gone limp; her eyes had rolled back in her head.

Jill Burfitt was in shock. This was all happening way too quickly. She wondered if screaming would help. As she thought about it, she vomited weakly down her blouse and on her shoes.

"Oh, that's just disgusting," Susanna's mother said in her real crack-whore voice. She looked twitchy and very unstable. "Now, Mrs. Burfitt," she continued in her Sgt. Adams' voice, "we only came here to get our baby girl back. If you scream, Susanna here loses an eye, then we kill you, and then we take Susanna anyway." Jill trembled, looking sideways at Susanna and her father.

"Now, you just nod your head yes, if you understand. No screaming, full cooperation, everybody stays safe. Yes?"

Jill nodded weakly.

"Like I always say, 'Fear is a great motivator,'" Susanna's father grated out. The young girl's breathing was shallow. She looked like she was there in body, but had willed her spirit to go elsewhere.

"Take her phone, you stupid bitch," Susanna's father said to his wife. *Girlfriend?*

Jill weakly handed her phone to the woman. The woman then dropped it on the floor and stomped on it until it no longer resembled a phone.

"Now use that duct tape we brought, and tape this old woman into that chair," Susanna's father directed. Susanna's mother brought over a small Windsor chair and Jill sat it in, meekly, shaking, still breathing raggedly.

"Put your hands on your legs, please, Mrs. Burfitt," Sgt. Adams/Susanna's mother was saying. Jill obliged, never taking her eyes off Susanna. She threw up again slightly.

"Okay, now I told you already—that is disgusting." The crack whore who claimed to be Susanna's mother roughly starting taping off Jill's mouth. She did three circles around Mrs. Burfitt's head with the tape, covering her mouth completely, then bit the tape and tore it off.

Susanna still isn't moving, Jill thought.

"Now tape her into the chair, you stupid bitch," Susanna's father directed.

Jill could see needle tracks on the woman's arms, hands, legs, as the skinny woman started at her shoulders, walking complete loops around Jill and the chair. "You shouldn't call me a stupid bitch in front of the girl," Susanna's mother protested irritably to her boyfriend. *Husband?* "How is that child ever going to have respect for me if you keep calling me a stupid bitch in front of her?"

"The man's laugh was rough and raspy. "Respect? Bitch, you need to look in a mirror. I'll cut off your candy supply, and you will be begging for a taste by sundown. You just keep tapin', and don't worry about any respect."

The threat of being cut off whatever it was she needed silenced the woman. After about fifteen circles, Jill was tightly taped from waist to shoulders to a chair in her upstairs bedroom. She was having quite a bit of difficulty breathing though her nose.

"Susanna, honey," the man was saying sweetly. He had taken his hand off her mouth and was slapping her lightly. "Wake up now—you're gonna come away with Mommy and Daddy." The little girl remained catatonic, pale, breathing shallowly.

Susanna's not there, Jill was thinking. *She's gone somewhere else.*

Susanna's father changed tactics. His voice went from sweet to Satanic: raspy, dirty, sick. Jill knew she'd never be able to get that voice out of her head.

"Susanna, you wake up now or I'll start cutting and burning this old woman. He held his knife near Jill's eye now, and with his other hand he pulled out a lighter and flicked it to a flame. "You remember Mr. Knife and Mr. Lighter, don't you, Susanna?"

The little girl's eyes flickered open, and she trembled a bit as her spirit re-entered her body.

***

Meanwhile, in Ottawa, Elijah had a message for the Canadian people from the House of Commons. CPAC had carried it live, as was their recent custom, and in terms of drama, the message did not disappoint.

Elijah had let his hair grow out lately—*like his girlfriend, the minister of youth?* People who wondered about such things were speculating. The same people said later he was dressed and looked like Jimi Hendrix on the cover of *Are You Experienced?* if you want a visual reference.

"Good afternoon. As you know, our current Canadian government has been a very vocal opponent of the Trimp administration. The president of the United States has surrounded himself with a Cabinet filled with climate-change deniers, uninformed billionaires and environmental rapists. Any Act or law that previously protected the American or global environment has been repealed. The United States has walked away from the valuable global agreements and carbon reduction targets reached at the Rio, Kyoto and Paris environmental summits.

"The US Department of Energy and the US Department of the Interior have been criminally negligent since January 20, 2017. American corporations have been drilling unsafely for gas and oil in previously protected US and international waters on an unprecedented level."

Viewers saw multiple spills on the map: Gulf of Mexico, Gulf of Maine, Alaskan Panhandle…

"Spills of oil and gas, on land and at sea, have risen 165 per cent during this current administration's watch."

Viewers saw a map of US pipeline leaks of oil and gas since 2017.

"The open-pit coal mines that this administration reopened to curry political favour in the Appalachian Mountains and river valleys have taken a catastrophic environmental and human toll."

Viewers saw scarred barren landscape with rivers full of floating dead fish.

"Unsafe fracking practices have increased more than 300 per cent since the Trimp administration took power. These practices have poisoned a vast amount of the water contained in the Central Plains Aquifer."

Viewers saw pictures of grassy plains in North Dakota, Wyoming and Montana from 2016. Cut to 2020—the same plains were now desert. Cut back to Elijah.

"Canada and the United States have been good neighbours for a long time. However, Canada can no longer sit idly by while the Trimp administration continues its criminal environmental assault on our planet. Much of the environmental damage that has occurred recently is directly affecting Canada and Canadians, due to our geographical proximity with the US. But this tragedy is not isolated within the boundaries of North America. The Trimp administration's energy policy—or lack thereof—is regarded as the largest threat to our planet today. Mr. Trimp, the damage you are doing in your greedy quest for fuel and money is endangering our whole planet, not just your own people.

"Therefore, the Government of Canada has no choice but to issue your administration an ultimatum. We demand that the United States government immediately return to global environmental summit meetings and commit in good faith to international target agreements regarding carbon reduction. We demand that the United States put back in place the Environmental Protections Agency with the authority and Acts that existed in 2016 prior to your administration."

The camera moved in closer on Elijah. "As an incentive to meet our demands quickly, we are raising the price of Canadian exports to America by 75 per cent on crude oil, natural gas, hydro-electricity and water. This price hike—you can call it a carbon tax if you like—is effective immediately. I should also advise you that the governments of Russia, Venezuela, Mexico, Brazil and Saudi Arabia are considering similar sanctions against your government. Mr. President, I look forward to your administration's commitment toward a sustainable planet."

Elijah's latest message broke the Internet. It was the lead story on every news channel in the world that had a six p.m. news show.

"We take you now to our correspondent in Washington, Donald MacNeil."

"Donald, how is the mood in Washington tonight after our prime minister's ultimatum?"

"Peter, this message is not being well received in Washington. Mr. Trimp is accustomed to giving ultimatums, but not to receiving them. I want to remind our viewers that this winter has been the harshest on record thus far for the eastern seaboard and the central United States. Record low temperatures have been broken in every state except Hawaii. Many of these states—in particular the New England states—have become increasingly reliant on Canadian fuel and electricity to heat their homes, schools and hospitals, run vehicles and power businesses. The Trimp administration is viewing these price increases on crude oil, natural gas, electricity and water at this time of year as criminal blackmail. President Trimp is holding an emergency meeting of his Cabinet as we speak. The White House press anticipates that President Trimp will deliver an emergency State of the Union Address within the hour."

Cut back to Peter.

"We'll return to Washington shortly. Next we take you to Manhattan. Our New York bureau chief is Milos

Ibrahimavic. He's been following the reaction to the prime minister's message at United Nations headquarters in New York City."

Cut to New York.

"Peter, the United Nations held a rare and unusual emergency meeting of the General Assembly following the Canadian prime minister's message to President Trimp. We'll take you to an address from the secretary general of the United Nations, Ingrid Aldisdottir. The taped segment our viewers are about to see took place approximately forty-five minutes ago."

"…The United Nations General Assembly is therefore resolved, by a vote of 186 to one, with nine nations abstaining. The General Assembly supports, in broad terms, the spirit and the intent of the Canadian prime minister's message to the government of the United States. The General Assembly of the United Nations wishes to encourage the government of the United States to return to global environmental summit meetings and commit to carbon reduction targets as quickly as possible."

Cut back to Peter.

"Milos, how unusual is it for the UN General Assembly to involve itself in what is basically a hard-ball trade dispute between two countries?"

"Well, the Charter of the United Nations states that 'the function of the General Assembly is to discuss, debate and make recommendations on a range of subjects pertaining to international peace and security, including development, disarmament, human rights, international law and peaceful arbitration between disputing nations.' I would suggest that the UN General Assembly might not have met if this was a cheese dispute between France and Switzerland. But today's message carried dangerous overtones. The General Assembly is well aware of the power of the United States from both an economical and military perspective. What was unusual was the overwhelming margin of votes in favour of this show of support. Traditionally, most NATO member countries would not vote against American interests in a resolution of this nature. In this matter however, the United States delegation was the sole opposing vote."

Cut back to Peter.

"That was Milos Ibrahimavic from the United Nations headquarters in Manhattan, New York."

***

Back in Maple Ridge, things were not good. Susanna's mom was carrying the little girl in her arms. Susanna was sucking her thumb and trembling. Just by the front door, the father stopped.

"Okay, listen carefully now, girls." Susanna's father was using the sweet voice again. "Daddy's gonna go out and start the car. When you hear the car start, you two come out. Easy, yes?"

Susanna's mother nodded emphatically. Susanna whispered, "Yes."

He almost opened the door and then paused as if remembering something.

"Oh, and Susanna—remember, honey—no screaming, or the nice lady upstairs meets Mr. Knife and Mr. Lighter. You don't want that, do you?"

Susanna whispered, "No."

Just as Susanna's father went out the door was when KT pulled her car in the driveway, blocking the exit point for Susanna and her alleged parents.

As KT got out of the car, she immediately sensed that something was very wrong indeed.

Who is this filthy creature walking toward me? she was thinking. *And where is Susanna?*

Susana's father was just as surprised by KT 's bad timing. He had put the knife in a back pocket and was reaching for it as he spoke. "Oh, hi. You must be K—"

He was cut off abruptly by the sound of breaking glass and KT's scream. The last thing he saw was a woman taped in a chair falling toward him. Jill Burfitt landed right on top of the man, and KT heard breaking bones, and a sickening thud. She was still screaming, but noticed neither her mother nor the man was moving. The man's neck seemed to be broken. They both looked dead.

"Where's Susanna?"

A scream from inside the house answered that question. KT bolted up the laneway and flung open the front door.

An emaciated and filthy creature was holding Susanna like a baby. Susanna looked pale, but conscious. "Now, you just back away from the door, and I'll take my natural born child and leave you in peace," the creature was saying in a surprisingly clear voice.

That was when Susanna buried her teeth in her mother's breast. The woman shrieked like a demon and tried to shake and slap Susanna free, but the child held on like a wolverine fighting a grizzly.

Acting on reflexes and adrenaline, KT punched the woman hard in the face, breaking the woman's nose.

The second punch caught her in the throat, and she fell to the ground making strangling noises, with Susanna still attached.

"Run, Susanna!" KT shouted. The child detached herself and spat out a mouthful of ripped flesh.

The creature was still moving, so KT just kept kicking it in the head. And kicking. And kicking.

When the police arrived moments later, they were horrified at what they saw. A young girl with a pretty big knife was literally butchering a man who was face-down in the driveway. He seemed to have been stabbed fifty to sixty times. Blood was running under two cars and into the street. She had almost completely severed his head, but was struggling to sever the vertebrae holding his head to his neck. She was not listening to the various orders from the police to put down the knife.

A female police officer approached quietly in the girl's field of vision and knelt about five feet in front of the little girl. The girl appeared to be hypnotized. She was whispering as she worked.

"Fear is a great motivator."

"Fear is a great motivator."

"Fear is a great motivator."

KT had heard the police cars arrive. She gave a couple more good stomps to what used to resemble a human skull, but now resembled something that had been roughly chopped in a blender.

Four policemen swung their revolvers toward KT as she came out the door.

"Put your hands in the air and get on your knees!" barked an officer through a megaphone.

KT raised her hands in the air, but kept walking.

"I'm that little girl's mother," KT shouted defiantly, as she walked toward Susanna. "So everybody just back off for a minute. Susanna!"

Susanna seemed to come out of her trance upon hearing KT's voice. She dropped the knife and ran into KT's outstretched arms.

A paramedic was kneeling by KT's mother. "This woman is still alive," he was shouting to the ambulance. There were at least seven police cars on the scene, and several officers helped the paramedics bring a stretcher to Mrs. Burfitt.

Four officers were holding back the neighbours from seeing things nobody should ever see. Two more officers were trying to secure the scene with yellow tape.

"Let me talk to those girls a minute please. That's my daughter and grand-daughter over there," Jill Burfitt whispered as the police and paramedics tried to cut her free from a chair.

A female officer brought KT to her mom.

"Oh, Momma, I thought you were dead." KT somehow found a reserve of new tears to cry.

"KT, us Burfitt girls don't die easy." She laughed dryly and coughed up some blood. "You look after that little girl, and remember that I love you both."

It got quiet for a minute inside KT's head.

Somewhere in the distance, a tea kettle was shrieking.

***

"Welcome back, viewers. We return now to Washington, where Donald MacNeil is standing by with an update."

"Peter, the White House press corps has indicated to foreign journalists that President Trimp has just finished an emergency meeting of his Cabinet, and that he will address the nation in approximately three minutes, in a live broadcast." As MacNeil spoke, security personnel could be seen in the background, herding journalists.

"White House security personnel have just directed all foreign journalists to sign off and to—" the CBC reporter's audio and video feed abruptly went blank. *Cut back to Peter Bridgeman.* He handled the unexpected pass with his normal dignity and aplomb.

"We'll have more from Washington in a moment when we re-establish our link with Donald MacNeil. For now, a word from our sponsors."

Peter Bridgeman and the Canadian Broadcasting Corporation were about to lose a whole bunch of viewers in the next three minutes. You see, Peter and most Canadians in the television industry were keenly aware of the following facts:

Eighty-five per cent of Canadians live within 160 kilometres of the US-Canada border.

That meant that for many years, Canadians watched more American television shows on American networks than Canadian productions on Canadian networks. Even back in the days of the rabbit ear antennae a lot of Canadian families near the border could capture one or two fuzzy US channels. When Canadian cable companies and then Canadian satellites started carrying American television shows on American networks, it became increasingly difficult to get Canadians to watch Canadian content.

"Whaddya wannna watch kids?"

"*The Beachcombers* or *Baywatch?*"

"*Don Messer's Jubilee* or *Ed Sullivan?*"

"*Reach For the Top* or *The Dukes of Hazard?*"

"*Mass for Shut-Ins* or *The Wonderful World of Disney?*"

"*The Littlest Hobo* or *The Bugs Bunny/Road Runner Hour?*"

"*The Canadian Women's Curling Championship* or *The SuperBowl?*"

Remember: over the years, the Canadian Radio-Television and Telecommunications Commission (*CRTC*) required that a certain percentage of all programs aired on Canadian radio and television stations had to have "Canadian content"—that is to say, they had to be made in Canada, for Canadians, about Canadians, by Canadians.

It was often said by CRTC executives and politicians that it was necessary for Canadians to watch and listen to Canadian content to avoid cultural assimilation by the United States, and to educate Canadians about their Canadian culture, history and heritage.

"Sure. I'll get right on that," the average Canadian thought.

"Right after I finish seeing if Bo and Luke Duke can rescue cousin Daisy and those bodacious ta-tas of hers from that pickle she's in with Roscoe and Boss Hogg…"

In a nutshell, American television had always had more…stuff. Their larger population = more viewers = more advertising revenue = higher production quality, more special effects…and more sex appeal.

The Mouse Who Poked an Elephant ∗ 219

Let's be honest. American television was sexier, more violent and more fun to watch than its conservative Canadian counterpart.

Since Elijah's election, however, viewership on CPAC (Canadian Public Affairs Channel) had increased significantly as Canadians tuned in to watch the best reality show ever. Seriously. People around the world were watching Canada's Parliament operate on TV.

But besides Canada's recent success with *Canadian Parliament—Live!* and reruns of *The Trailer Park Boys* in Australia, Canadian content on television scored pretty low in the Neilsen ratings—both in Canada, and abroad.

All of these thought were racing through Peter Bridgeman's head as the make-up people freshened him up during the commercial break. "Can we carry a live feed of the president's address?" he asked the show's producers. *I already know the answer, but I have to ask.*

"No. C'mon Peter, you know how the game is played. We are the Canadian Broadcasting Corporation, not the American Broadcasting Corporation. We'll report on what the president says a few minutes after he wraps it up. In the interim, we'll run that story about the university kids who built that cool solar-powered car."

"And we are live in three, two, one…"

"Welcome back to *The National*. The president of the United States is speaking to Americans in an emergency State of the Union Address that begins in one minute. We'll have more coverage on that address and how it will affect Canadians, near the top of the hour. For our next story, we are going to the University of Manitoba, where a group of electrical engineering students have…"

Of the 2.35 million Canadians who had been watching the CBC news, 2.25 million switched to an American network. The remaining viewers still watching the CBC were likely asleep or too geographically isolated to get an American channel.

"A MESSAGE FROM THE PRESIDENT OF THE UNITED STATES…"

President Trimp, as was customary, appeared to be simultaneously furious, bewildered, and deeply insulted.

"Good evening, my fellow Americans. Recently, the Canadian prime minister issued an ultimatum to the government of the United States.

"In that ultimatum, the Canadian prime minister—who is a real punk and a big loser, by the way—has demanded that we agree to follow the findings of global climate scientists and agree to significant carbon target reductions.

"If we do not agree to their ridiculous demands, the Canadian government is threatening to place a 75 per cent increase on the cost of the fossil fuels, electricity and water, which the United States currently purchases from Canada through internationally recognized trade agreements."

Zoom-in on Trimp.

"Mr. Prime Minister—and the rest of you Canuckleheads up there in Soviet Canuckistan that are watching this—the United States does not bend to ultimatums or blackmail from any nation.

"In response, here is a list of our demands.

"Your prime minister and his ridiculous band of tree-hugging communists will rescind your ultimatum, and apologize to the people of the United States and—most importantly—to me.

"You will demand that the United Nations rescind their recent thoughtless comments regarding the United States' commitment to carbon reduction.

"Finally, your country *will* continue to provide the United States with fossil fuels, hydo-electricity and water at the current market rates as described in our various trade agreements."

Zoom back out, show multiple massive military forces in the background and the POTUS in the foreground: tanks, planes, aircraft carriers, ground troops, artillery pieces, stealth fighters, frigates, battleships and nuclear submarines all bustling about and blowing shit up in various foreign locations.

"Mr. Prime Minister, if you fail to meet our demands within the next thirty-six hours, the United States of America will have no choice but to annex your country.

"Your provinces and territories will become states. We think maybe six states, but we'll figure that out as we go. Our team has a plan, and it'll be a great plan.

"Your citizens who surrender peacefully, will, in time, be allowed the great honour of becoming American citizens.

"Those who oppose us will be considered enemies of the United States of America. We will use all necessary military force to achieve this goal."

Zoom in on the POTUS (looking slightly more unstable than normal but still making his signature "thumb and index finger together in a circle" gesture—it normally signified important speaking points to the Trimpanzees).

"Mr. Prime Minister, it's your move. You tried to punk the Punk Master? There can only be one winner here, and his name is Donald J. Trimp. Remember, I never ever lose.

Ask Mallory Clifton if you don't believe me. You have thirty-six hours to submit to my ultimatum.

"To the people of the United States—take heart. I will not let you freeze in the dark. May God continue to bless America."

***

Elijah and his Cabinet watched the president's address on NBC. The mood in the room was sombre. "All right, as we predicted, The Donald is not amused." Elijah stood up, and stretched. "So, we've come this far. I say we shut 'em down. Do any of you disagree?"

The room was quiet. "I'm gonna take your silence as assent." Elijah began to pace around the room as was his custom.

"So. Harjit, are we ready to activate the Emergency Measures Act?" Harjit Singh was a large Sikh with significant combat and intelligence gathering experience in the Middle East and Afghanistan. As a former infantry colonel, he was well respected by his troops in the regular force and the militia.

"Ready when you are, my friend. Say the word, and we'll activate our militia."

"Tim, you were gonna find out how quickly we can shut down the seven main oil pipelines to the US."

Tim Barr was Canada's minister of environment and climate change. "Keystone is the biggest. It would take twenty-four hours to safely turn off that tap, and shut down the pumping and transfer stations. The other eight can be closed within eighteen hours."

Elijah was poised with another question, but his energy minister anticipated the question and beat him to the punch. "The gas pipelines are quicker—there are nine main lines, and thirteen tributaries. They can be switched off within eight hours."

"And the hydro we supply from various points?"

"As we discussed last week, that one is the easiest to turn off. You tell us the time, it's done in five seconds.

"Okay. I want your people at each location working with our Armed Forces security members who've been training for this operation. Let's make sure we do this safely and smartly—no spills. Have your teams begin turning off the taps at 0005 this morning.

"Harjit, I want yourself and the chief of defence staff with me when we make the Emergency Measures announcement. In the rotunda at midnight?"

"Very good, sir."

"Questions? Yes, Tim?"

"Are we turning off the trans-America water pipeline to the southwestern states? As per last week's brief, that's a lot of people with very low water reserves."

Elijah thought for a minute, then shook his head.

"Let's save that card in case we need to play it later in the game."

CHAPTER 15.
Faint Hope Clause

When studying the Trimp dynasty, most historians speculate that Elijah's announcement from Parliament was the tipping point that sent President Donald Trimp hurtling from the "embarrassing buffoon" category into the "certifiably and criminally insane" category.

Still others said that The Donald's horrifying descent into madness was the compounded result of thousands of satirical *Saturday Night Live* sketches, multiplied by the hundreds of millions of satirical posts, which had slammed him on every social media platform imaginable for the past five years.

Many renowned psychologists and psychiatrists have hypothesized that President Trimp suffered from extreme narcissism. In laymen's terms, he desperately needed to know that people loved and respected him, and that he was the most important person in the world. In even baser laymen's terms, The Donald was the biggest attention whore the world had ever witnessed. It was absolutely essential for his mental well-being that the attention was positive.

It is likely that when he was CEO of large companies (his pre-political era), thousands of his employees learned to enforce and indeed feed that massive ego, or... "You're fired."

By contrast, in most democratic systems, politicians learn the hard way that they work for the people, not vice versa. When Donald Trimp entered the political arena, he was stepping into territory where he had no experience; he had never ever been criticized or questioned by someone he could not control. And the pressure of that exponentially increasing criticism from people he could not silence or shut down eventually caused him to go mad.

Whatever the cause for his eventual collapse, most historians, journalists and songwriters generally agree on the events as described below.

Elijah did a brief broadcast to the world from the House of Commons at midnight on January 21, 2021. He was accompanied by a large Indian man in a turban, who was introduced as the Canadian minister of national defence, and a very professional looking female admiral, who was introduced as chief of the defence staff.

Trimp, according to reliable sources who watched the broadcast with him, was "astonished that any government would even appoint an Indian and a woman to positions of such esteem."

Elijah began his announcement by apologizing to the American people for what he felt he had to do.

He went on to say that the Canadian government needed to turn off the pipelines that provided oil and gas to US refineries in order to make the POTUS see the error of his ways regarding his administration's lack of concern for the planet's environment.

Elijah further explained that he, regrettably, needed to shut down the hydro-electricity that powered much of the New England states, as well. "And if your president does something aggressive in a military manner against Canada, I will also need to turn off the trans-American pipeline that is providing water to the southwest US."

"So, look. I love you guys, and I don't wanna hurt anybody, but sometimes leaders have to make tough decisions. And this is that time."

Elijah wrapped it up by inviting all the people in America who needed food, shelter and warmth to come to Canada.

"Our militia, our border services personnel, our police forces, our emergency services personnel and, most importantly, millions of Canadian citizens, are standing by to help you if you want to come to Canada. We only ask that you do not bring firearms. I promise you, you won't need them. Rumours of wild moose attacks in our country are merely urban myths.

"We will welcome you to our country with open arms. We will put you up in our homes, our schools, our hospitals and public buildings. Hey, please don't forget the no guns part—it's a really big deal for us. Good night, neighbours. We love you guys. Sorry for this."

At 0005 on January 22, it went dark in a lot of New England and many of the Great Lakes states. It's estimated that the power outage affected sixty-five million Americans.

At 01:00 the same morning, natural gas pressure in a lot of pipelines in those same states began to drop quickly. By 08:00 most natural gas utilities—furnaces for heating, stoves for cooking and gas-fired electrical generating stations—were not working.

Governors and senators in those states most affected were scrambling to call out their emergency response teams. Phones were ringing off multiple hooks across the USA (not that many phones still had hooks, but the older readers will know what I mean).

Mayors of every town and city were calling their state leaders looking for help in providing warmth and shelter for their citizens.

By 14:00, the US-Canada border was packed with cars, RVs and school buses. President Trimp (who reportedly saw tweets of the crowded border crossings), ordered the border closed for Americans crossing into Canada. If the American border service agents got the message at a headquarters level, it didn't make it down to the agents working the 172 manned border crossings that spanned the various borders between the two countries.

The Canadian and US border officials were working pretty well together, just like they always had. The border between various Canadian provinces and their neighbouring states is 8891 kilometres long (that's 5525 miles for our American friends.) So the people entering Canada through the 172 manned crossing sites were a drop in the bucket.

There were literally a thousand more places where you just had to go to the library, walk across a creek, or a ditch, or a wheat field, and you had left the US and entered Canada (and vice versa of course).

At each crossing point, militia soldiers and police forces helped direct their American neighbours to nearby hotels where they could warm up and get a bite to eat. Still others who had no vehicles were put in school buses and shuttled to Canadian military bases, local schools, arenas and university dorms.

Thousands of Canadians were showing up at the borders from the Atlantic to the Pacific to greet people and offer them space in their homes.

Enterprising fishermen from ports in Maine, Alaska and Washington were loading up people in their fishing boats and dropping them off in New Brunswick and northern and southern British Columbia. Still others walked or drove across the frozen Great Lakes and the hundreds of rivers and tributaries that the two countries shared.

But all that was happening only for the Americans who lived near the Canadian border. A lot of other people were just plain cold, scared and really angry.

***

Meanwhile in Washington, it was zero degrees Celsius (okay, thirty-two degrees Fahrenheit for our American readers) but the wind chill made it feel much colder. An angry mob was descending on the White House and other Capitol buildings, which still had emergency heat and lights from underground generating stations. That only made people madder.

Reports indicate that White House security shot the first 327 people who tried to breach the White House fence. Eventually, the mob's combined mass and weight breached the fence and there wasn't enough security to keep shooting that many people. Also, in accordance with their Second Amendment right to bear arms, many citizens had begun to return fire.

The White House was under attack by its own citizens. (Readers should be reminded that it's called the "White House" because of the white paint used after it suffered damage from a fire at the hands of British troops and Canadian militiamen in 1814.)

A few minutes after the White House fence had been breached, multiple helicopter gunships flew in over the White House. On their first run, they strafed the crowd killing hundreds of people, and injuring another several thousand. The gunships had now moved on and were strafing a circle that measured about a kilometre (oh, for heaven's sakes: point-six-two of a mile) in diameter around the White House.

A voice over a loudspeaker addressed the crowd. "This is Maj. Gen. Vance Cartwright. Washington, DC, is under martial law by order of the president of the United States. You are hereby under arrest. If anyone resists, we will deploy the gunships again. You will lie face down on the ground until you are arrested."

At that moment, thousands of Marines in full battle gear burst out from all parts of the White House and descended on the mob.

Vice president Mike Pens came out on the Truman balcony, flanked by a lot of very well armed Marines. The Vice President and Maj. Gen. Cartwright were behind bulletproof glass shields.

"Where is President Trimp?" shouted a lonely voice near the balcony.

Maj. Gen. Cartwright looked at the vice president quizzically, then handed him the loudspeaker.

"President Trimp's location is a matter of national security," the vice president answered.

A female voice answered from the lawn near the balcony.

"That's funny 'cause he just tweeted something. Listen—from his @ POTUS account.

"At Pentagon. Kiss your sorry asses good bye, Canada. Nuclear attack headed your way in sixty seconds."

Maj. Gen. Cartwright did a facepalm for a few seconds, then took the megaphone back from the vice president. "This is Maj. Gen. Cartwright again. I want to assure you that President Trimp will not be launching a nuclear attack, now, or at any time in the future."

"Why should we believe you?" asked the female voice on the lawn.

"Because we decided five years ago that he was far too mentally unstable to be trusted with nuclear codes."

This news infuriated Vice President Pens. "Gen. Cartwright, if what you are saying is true, you have placed our country in tremendous danger. We could be under nuclear attack at any time by the Canadians. Marines, arrest Maj. Gen. Cartwright on charges of treason."

The Marines looked at each other uncertainly, but made no move to arrest the general.

The Vice President was shouting now. "Marines, arrest this general or I will have you all arrested for treason."

Gen. Cartwight weighed his options for a moment, then decided someone needed to break the stalemate. He had been a gold gloves boxer, back in the day, and would have represented the US Olympic team in 1980 if the games in Moscow hadn't been boycotted. He still took considerable pride in maintaining a high level of fitness.

All of this was evident to the people on the White House lawn. Those who saw the punch said it was a classic left uppercut. Vice President Pens was not one of those witnesses: he never saw the punch coming. It knocked him out colder than a codfish.

Cartwright was a man used to making quick decisions. That was on full display over the next few minutes.

"Marines—attenhut!"

One thousand members of the Marine Corps snapped to attention all over the White House lawn.

"Listen up, Marines. Belay my last order to arrest these people. Delta Company, free those citizens that have been arrested thus far. Alpha, Bravo and Charlie Company, start treating the wounded."

The general barked more orders into a radio, and the gunships turned and slowly pulled away from the mob in Washington, DC.

Meanwhile, at the Pentagon, in the room with the highest levels of security in the world, President Donald Trimp clarified with his chiefs of staff that the entire United States arsenal of nuclear weapons was directed at every Canadian town with more than 15,000 people.

"President Trimp, I'm not sure we need to fire our entire nuclear arsenal at Canada. I mean, that is enough nuclear power to destroy the whole planet several hundred times over."

"Admiral, trust me, I know what I'm doing," President Trimp interrupted. "I know more about nuclear weapons than all of you."

An Air Force general (who held a doctorate in nuclear engineering) tried his luck next. "Sir, what if we just do a tactical nuclear strike on one city? Like Winnipeg, for example? I have a sister married to a Canadian and she lives in Winnipeg. She says it would be like a mercy killing, and most Canadians wouldn't even miss it. Then you could convince the Canadian prime minister to—"

"I'm done talking to the Canadian prime minister, general. The time for talk is past—this is a time for action. Let's prepare to launch. Talk me through this. My code, then red button, or…?"

The Donald was pacing now, crackling with enthusiasm at the task at hand.

Gen. "Pit Bull" Pruitt was the president's favourite of the three chiefs of staff. The feeling was by no means mutual. It was believed by many that the president just liked the fact that he had a tough guy named "Pit Bull" in his stable.

"Sir, our intelligence reports indicate that there are currently one-point-seven million Americans who just entered Canada over the past few hours, and another one hundred million American citizens who will be killed by fallout from the blast within forty-eight hours."

"Chiefs of Staff, that's enough. I've made up my mind. Those Americans in Canada now are traitors, and I won't be needing their help to make America great again. As your commander in chief, this is a direct order. We will now wipe Canada off the face of the earth."

The chiefs of staff looked at each other grimly.

"Aye, aye, sir," said the admiral. "So, here's the launch sequence." President Trimp was beyond delighted, rubbing his hands together with obvious anticipation.

The admiral directed the president to a chair in front of a big red button labelled "launch."

"All right, Mr. President. It takes four codes in the correct sequence to launch a nuclear strike—one from each chief of staff plus you as commander in chief. As discussed when you were elected, we have done this to prevent a madman from destroying the world, singlehandedly."

"Great idea, terrific planning," interjected the president. The chiefs of staff had never seen him look happier.

"So, first, Gen. Pruitt will enter his code…" As the general typed, the words appeared on a screen above them.

"QWERTY?" the president asked. "Pit Bull's code is QWERTY?"

"Yes, sir—I use it as a password for everything. It's just easy for me to remember, and hackers would never guess to use it."

"Right. Smart. Terrific. Good job, Pit Bull. Okay, Admiral, who's next?"

"Air Force!" responded Gen. Saxon. "DO, RE, MI, ABC, 123…" the general hummed as he typed it in.

"Wait, isn't that a song by the Jackson Five?" President Trimp asked.

"It sure is, sir," Saxon responded. "It was one of their first hits. I was in a Jackson Five cover band back in the day, sir, so I'll never forget the password."

"Who were you in the band? Were you Michael, or…?"

"No, sir. I was too big to be Michael. I was Germaine—he got way more girls than Michael anyways."

The president loved that line. "Ha! Good thinking!" he shouted (a little too enthusiastically). "Go for the pussy—always!" The president was having so much fun he had to stop and wipe away some tears. "God, I love spending time with you guys. We gotta do this more often…wait—so who was Michael?"

"My little sister played Michael, sir. She had the moves, the voice, everything."

"She sounds delightful," Trimp interjected. "Where is she now?"

"She's the sister in Winnipeg, sir."

"Mmm. Tough break. Okay, Adm. McHale. Batter up!"

"Indeed, sir."

THE_END_ IS_ NIGH, Adm. McHale typed.

"What's that mean, Admiral? President Trimp asked. "Were you in a band, as well? 'Cause that's a great name for a band."

"No, sir. This password has tremendous meaning for me. It signifies that if we unleash nuclear weapons, it could signal the end of the wor—"

"Awww—what a buzzkill!" Trimp shouted, punching the admiral playfully. "Really. I mean way to harsh our buzz, Admiral. Sheesh."

"Sir, the commander in chief always has the final call," Gen. Pruitt was saying. "We can stand down and discuss other options, or…"

"C'mon, you guys are getting all serious on me. As commander in chief, we are launching."

The Mouse Who Poked an Elephant ⁎ 235

"Sir, if you're committed to launching, you just enter your password, then hit the 'launch' button," Adm. McHale explained.

"Okay. And what's my password?"

"I'll give you a hint, sir. Four years ago when you assumed the presidency, you chose it based on a catchy T-shirt slogan for your Democratic opponent."

"Ooooo, oooo—I remember now!"

TRIMP_THAT_BITCH! President Trimp entered.

The generals and staff officers in the launch chamber looked grim.

"It's still not too late, sir. We can turn back without launching and discuss other—"

It was too late. President Donald Trimp had firmly and aggressively brought his hand down on the "launch" button.

The room was sombre.

"I don't hear anything," President Trimp said. "Shouldn't there be rocket noises, or…?"

The chiefs of staff, and those other military members entrusted with the mightiest arsenal ever known, couldn't take it anymore.

The people in the room exploded in laughter, people were rollin' on the floor…

"Wait—what's the joke?" The POTUS didn't like being the only guy not in the joke.

"He, he, he thinks we actually gave him nuclear codes…" The admiral was laughing so hard he could barely breathe.

"It's like a time-delay thing, right? It's like an inside joke you guys play on all the presidents. In a minute there'll be a big whooooosh, and…?" President Trimp was turning an unusual shade of crimson.

"BWAHAHAHAHAHAHAHAHAHAHAHA HAHAHA!"

These new questions just made the group laugh twice as hard. If that was even physically possible. Every single person interviewed from the launch chamber after the incident said it was the hardest they had ever laughed in their lives.

"I have a grandson I would trust with the codes before this man, "McHale wheezed. The crowd tried to catch their breath. "And he's three years ol—".

"BWAHAHAHAHAHAHAHAHAHAHAHA HA!"

The POTUS had heard enough. "All right!" he shouted. "I. WANT. THESE. NUCLEAR. WEAPONS. LAUNCHED. RIGHT. NOW!" With each word he pounded on the "launch" button.

The room watched him quietly for a minute.

"BWAHAHAHAHAHAHAHAHAHAHAHA HAHAHAHAHAHAHA!"

"Mr. President, there's a tweet you should see from the Canadian prime minister." The room went quiet as "Pit Bull" Pruitt passed the POTUS a phone.

"You should read it aloud, sir. It's important information we should all hear."

Trimp cleared his throat and assumed his presidential stance.

"It says, '@POTUS—when should we expect that nuclear strike? We've been waiting patiently. @elijah.'"

"BWAHAHAHAHAHAHAHAHAHAHAHA HA!"

If possible, this enraged President Trimp even more.

"I gotta stop laughing soon," an older chief petty officer cried/wheezed to McHale. "My heart won't—"

All eyes swivelled as the old master chief hit the deck. "Medic!"

There is nothing like someone having a heart attack to get a group to stop laughing.

While two medics delivered CPR to the chief, "Pit Bull" Pruitt and Adm. McHale ordered the arrest of President Trimp. The military police gently stopped him from thumping the "launch" button...

"Make sure he has medical care twenty-four seven," McHale told the colonel in charge of the president's security.

"Aye, aye, sir." The colonel saluted smartly.

All the military personnel in the launch room were investigated by FBI and CIA personnel.

"I actually pissed myself," one military police officer admitted during his interview. "I mean, I was laughing so hard I lost control of my bladder and just kept pissing myself for, like, thirty seconds. Look, here it comes on the tape. See that piss stain spreading? I mean I ain't proud of it but my goodness that was funny."

"Oh heavens, yes—it was the funniest thing ever," the arresting officer agreed. "But also sad at the end. I mean, here we are arresting our commander in chief, and he was still trying to tweet a reply to the Canadian prime minister, and look there on the tape—that's a big piss stain on Sgt. Oliver's leg."

At 04:00 on January 22, Vice President Pens was still in a coma, and his jaw was broken. He had hit his head on the floor of the Truman balcony when Gen. Cartwright had hit him. White House medical staff were quoted as saying that there could be long-term brain damage as a result of the trauma.

"Nah, he had that long before the trauma," tweeted his many opponents.

"Too soon?" tweeted others in reply.

At 5:00 a.m. on January 22, the Speaker of the House, Ryan Paul, called the Canadian prime minister.

"This is the minister of youth," Juliette answered.

"May I speak with the Canadian prime minister, please?"

"Elijah, it's for you," she shouted into the shower.

Juliette listened in as the Canadian prime minister spoke with the Speaker of the House of Representatives.

According to US constitutional law, if both the president or vice president were incapacitated (unable to function for medical reasons or death) or impeached, the Speaker of the House was next in line as commander in chief.

"So I can assure you Mr. Prime Minister that under my direction as temporary commander in chief, the United States will in fact commit to global environmental carbon reduction targets. Essentially, we are giving you what you requested in your ultimatum to President Trimp."

The line was quiet for a moment while Elijah pondered this.

Elijah then explained politely to Ryan Paul that this wasn't enough.

"Look, you guys have a chance for a fresh start here. If we do what you are suggesting, you're still stuck with a Cabinet full of Trimp's billionaire friends. I have an alternate proposal for you. Please hear me out—and then try to sell it as your idea."

The Speaker of the House patiently listened while Elijah explained his plan.

In the end, after thirty minutes of reasonable debate, Ryan Paul reluctantly said, "It's worth a shot, but we have to discuss it in the House of Representatives and the Senate."

"Ryan, you and I both know that will require about nine months of arguing and, at the end of those nine months, you will have only widened the divide in your country. Dude, carpe diem. Just do it—you are the president. I mean it's your call, but I'm not turning any taps back on to anything unless we see the result we just discussed."

At 8:00 p.m. Eastern Standard Time on January 22, Ryan Paul, the temporary president of the United States of America addressed the nation. It was the largest television audience in the world to date.

During his address, the Speaker noted that America had been a nation divided since President Trimp's election.

"...Both President Trimp and Vice President Pens are currently not able to fulfil their oaths of office. According to our Constitution, that means that I will act as the president until such time as the president or vice president are able to resume their duties. I am deeply honoured to act in this capacity."

Ryan Paul spoke from the heart (but in a good way, not an incoherent angry Trimpian way).

"Look, I want to be honest with you. And I know that we haven't always been honest with you, and, for that, many of the elected officials in our once proud Republican Party are deeply embarrassed and ashamed."

He highlighted the ugly political divide that had widened over the past four years.

"…A divide that pitted left against right, Democrat against Republican, Christian against Muslim, whites against non-whites, rich against poor, rural against urban, straights against the LGBTQ community, strong against weak, healthy against the infirm…"

He spoke at length of the international damage that Donald Trimp's administration had done over the past four years.

"…Alienating and belittling our traditional allies…

"Willfully denying science in the name of profit, and carelessly exploiting natural resources at a pace that has done immeasurable environmental damage…

"For my part in this administration's role, I can tell you that I am deeply ashamed of my actions, and the actions of the Republican Party over the past four years.

"In January 2017, President Trimp buried reports from the CIA and FBI that Russian intelligence agencies interfered in the last US election, willfully ignored any facts which were not favourable toward his retention of power, and had his team of spin doctors and con men invent fictional facts and figures to bury the truth.

"Therefore, in my first act as president of the United States, I am placing former President Trimp and former Vice President Pens under arrest for conspiracy against the United States of America. Their hearings will be held as soon as each of them is declared medically fit to stand trial."

It was an emotionally draining broadcast. Ryan Paul was an organized, thoughtful, meticulous and experienced litigator and politician.

"As the results of our last election were tainted, I therefore declare null and void all those appointments made by former president Trimp.

"This includes all secretaries of state, ambassadors, judicial appointments…

"We will fill these vacant positions and appointments with the most qualified persons, based on recommendations from a committee consisting of ten Senators from the Democratic Party and ten Senators from the Republican Party."

Ryan Paul ended his broadcast on a high note. He explained that another US election was slated for Nov 3, 2020. He encouraged the American people to consider independent candidates, or at least moderate members of either major established party.

"We have been doing the same things for a while now. But as someone who has been part of this system for some time, I need to tell you that our current political system is broken. We are divided by partisan politics, by left and right, by our parties' platforms.

"We elect Republicans to fix a Democratic mess, and four years later we elect Democrats to fix a Republican mess. We are doing the same things over and over, and expecting different results."

In blacked-out homes and buildings all across the New England and Great Lake states, lights began to flicker on.